There's Nothing Like a Woman Scorned

A WOMEN'S COURAGE TO ENDURE SUFFERING FOR THE SAKE OF LOVE!

DAWNA DURHAM

authorHOUSE®

AuthorHouse™
1663 Liberty Drive
Bloomington, IN 47403
www.authorhouse.com
Phone: 833-262-8899

Published by AuthorHouse 07/16/2020

ISBN: 978-1-7283-6616-6 (sc)
ISBN: 978-1-7283-6615-9 (e)

Library of Congress Control Number: 2020912051

Print information available on the last page.

This book is printed on acid-free paper.

I'm not your door mat

I'm not your door mat
you just can't walk on me
then expect me to be
all I can be.

I have taken in everything
you can wipe on me.
You punch me and slap me
you do everything to hurt me.

Than you turn around
and want to make love to me.
After you're done, you fall asleep on me.

I'm not your door mat,
I'm better than that,
I'm the one who held your hand,
I made you my main man,
I helped you get back on your feet,
you think you can say and do what you want.

Who do you think you are,
you just can't piss on me
than set me aside to dry my eyes.
You see, I soaked it all in
dried it up and spit it back out.

I'm a strong sister
I stuck threw it to the bitter end,
but after today,
this story will end
I'm not your door mat.

-Dawna Durham

Beaten

Daily,
You have beaten me, I am bruised.
I cry and I cry.
Nightly,
You have rapped me; you have taken me, forcefully.
I cry and I cry.
Internally,
You have destroyed me; torn me to shreds.
I cry and I cry.
You whisper,
I love you; if you leave your dead.
I cry and I cry.
For I have feared to speak my truths.
Dead…am I.

-M.R.D.J

Be Aware
A Women's Smile and Laughter,
Can be the shield that hides her Truths

- M.R.D.J

CONTENTS

Acknowledgments xi

Chapter 1 The Beginning 1
Chapter 2 Business as usual 6
Chapter 3 The night we meet 13
Chapter 4 The morning after 21
Chapter 5 At the store 30
Chapter 6 The night that changed everything 35
Chapter 7 Nothing but smiles 46
Chapter 8 The right things to say 53
Chapter 9 Six months later 61
Chapter 10 The verbal and physical abuse continues 67
Chapter 11 The heat is on 74
Chapter 12 The Heat continues 82
Chapter 13 The rage 88
Chapter 14 The Rage Continues 94

Crisis Services 103
About the Author 105

Acknowledgments

I'd like to take a moment and give thanks to those who have believed in my dedication to bring awareness to those suffering in silence.

To Mindy DeJesus, co-author of There's nothing like a Women Scorned. You are indeed a rare individual who without reservation, assist me more than I can thank you for Many Blessing my friend.

To Author House who helped me publish this book. Thank you for believing in the cause.

To my best friend, I miss you every day. I wish I could have heard your unspoken truths. I wish I could have seen past your beautiful smile and infectious laughter. My heart aches to think you were suffering alone. I pray every day that even one person will find the courage to speak up and fight for a better tomorrow. One day we will meet again, until then I'll hold you close to my heart. May God keep you eternally in his glory!

Chapter One

The Beginning

It all started off one day when I was sitting and minding my business at club Magic. The music was just right. My rum and coke was on point. Needless to say, I was too. I had my red thigh high boots on, with my black fitted dress and yes honey my red purse. Can you say fab-u-lous? I have all eyes on me.

You see me; I'm not out here looking for anyone. I'm just here to have a little fun after working all week. Besides, if you meet a man in a club, he's bond to go and find another chic in the next club. There's no real love up in here. So I stand clear from the fuckery. I just sit back and laugh at the scenery.

As I sit here sipping on my nice cold drink I notice that some of these ladies be cutting up on the dance floor, asses all up on different men. Hands on places they shouldn't be unless they plan on putting out later.

I can't help but sit back and wonder what the fuck their doing? Not to mention, what in the hell their wearing?

Seriously, your friend didn't tell you that your clothes look Jacked up or that you look like a fucking hot mess. Shit, she isn't a real friend.

Let my friends come out with me looking like a hot ass mess. First thing out my mouth would be, "I know you don't think you're going with me looking like that. You better take your ass back in the house and come back out in some other clothes". I don't play that you're not going to be around here embarrassing me, nor yourself.

While my thoughts consume me, I notice a tall dark figure approach from behind me. Damn! I'm greeted with a fine ass brother. That's until he opens his mouth "Dam, girl where's the extinguisher cause you on fire. Can I buy you a drink?"

About too act a fool and tells this man about himself, I politely say, "no thank you"! Apparently he's used to rejection because he hits me with, "Oh come on baby. I can take care of you".

Men!! Do you think it's ok to keep harassing a woman in the club? No means No. Like what you don't get the N or the O, No!! With my nicest voice and a smile I repeat "no Thank you".

Turning in my seat to face away from him to check out the view, His response was a shock to my ears "Whatever you ungrateful bitch". What happens next is completely his fault of course. I told him no, a nice no too, but I guess that wasn't good enough and now he's name calling, So much for being polite. Here goes my mouth. I turn to face him and the rest is history.

"First off, you got that lame ass line from someone on social media. Get yourself a dictionary and put some words together so you can find yourself some new lines and how about go and take care of that breath. It's about to put me in a coma. Smelling like old trash from weeks ago. Gum can't help that shit. Might as well throw your teeth and gums away, and start all over again.

What you gone say, you ate some onions, how about the unions ate you. Get the fuck out of here with that shit".

Men be killing me with them whack ass lines and hot ass breath. Then have the nerve to call you out your name. Hell I tried to be nice. I know some call me crazy. I just call it keeping it real. Many don't understand that term, to busy faking the funk, trying to impress others. I guess it's time for me to move seeing as this fool hasn't left yet and I don't have the time or patience for stupidity.

Man this club is packed tonight. I make my way across the dance floor, drink in hand held high above the crowd so I don't spill any, which difficult seeing as I'm only about 5"4 with my heels on.

Finally, I manage to make my way through all the drunken sweaty bodies to the dimly lit booth in the back corner. Taking a seat, I wipe the sweat from my brow and take a sip of my drink.

Looking out at the sea of bodies I'm remember that I'm alone. Yes, I said I'm alone! My girlfriend didn't have a babysitter. So I'm chilling by myself. Not that I have a problem being alone. It's just that I can only talk so much shit to myself without looking crazy. Besides I'm happy I don't have those kinds of problems. You know the kind, KIDS!

I know I must sound like a real asshole, but I don't want any kids. Stretch marks, crying babies, finding a babysitter, Hell No! I'm not messing up my body, I'm sure as hell am not trying to have no kids working up my nerve and shit and I like my freedom.

Sleep hits me like sand in my face and my eyes begin to burn. I check my phone, Dam it's almost 2am. I need to get out of here so I can get to the office by 10 this morning.

I'm the owner of Sexy & Classy clothing store. Not trying to gloat but I'm doing very well for myself. I have people from all over buying my clothes. Who would have thought that I'd have my own business, especially one that's thriving?

In my younger years I thought I would have been a singer, As much as I like to sing. Guess that wasn't my calling, maybe in my next life. I finish my last few sips of rum and coke and make my way to the exit.

As I exit the club I can't help being relieved that the weather is still warm enough for me to enjoy it. I live less than ten minutes away on foot so I saved on gas tonight and walked. It's a good thing too, I'm feeling those drinks. While I make the short walk home, my thoughts overwhelm me.

Business in a couple of hours I wonder how much sleep I'm going to get. Especially thinking about some of my employees that be working on my dam nerve, with all them lame ass excuses on why they can't make it to work or have to leave early.

I've never heard so many people cry about not having a job or money, but aren't willing to put in the work on keeping and maintaining a job. How do they expect to survive like that? Don't they care about paying their bills, feeding their family etc.?

I'm getting a headache just thinking about it. So I rub my temples as I walk. Who am I to worry about that shit? Hell, I try my best to help.

I'm finally home time to try and sleep before I act a fool in the morning. I can't be acting evil and mess up my beauty sleep. Sleep time it is... By the way, my name is Aja.

Chapter Two

Business as usual

What feels like mere minutes since I closed my eyes, I begin to wake. Feeling the warmth of the sun filter in threw the window curtains; I roll over and look at the clock with squinted eyes. I sit up, OMG, its 9 am. I can't believe my alarm didn't go off, then again, I probably didn't hear it. That rum and coke sure put my ass out.

More exciting thoughts cross my mind. Now only if that was a man putting me out from all that nasty. Shit!!! I need a man's touch, just his touch, not his ass. Men are just trouble, and I don't have time for that. I'll just keep buying batteries for my fake ass dick that doesn't talk back, ask for anything, lie, or cheat on me. Only thing it needs is new AA batteries. I shake my head to stop thinking about all that good nasty sex I long for and get my ass to the store.

The warm and sunny day wakes me completely and offers some comfort. Feeling enthusiastic I enter work with a smile "Hello everyone! Today is Saturday. Let's make that money".

Sarah walks out from the back room with cloths in hand. "Morning Miss Aja, Tonya called off today" so much for my good mood. "What's her excuse today, Sarah?"

"She's sick with the flu". "Flu my ass, She went out I'm sure, and had one to many drinks. I hope that child knows that one more call off and she's gone. At least you came in today".

Frustrated, I turn to walk away. "Sarah, I'll be in my office, if you need me that is where I'll be. I have to get these web orders taken care of, so I'll be a while". "Ok Miss Aja, I'll try not to bother you". "Thank you Sarah"!

I can't help but be annoyed as fuck that Tonya called off again. She knows this is one of our busiest days.

Starring out my office window I vent to myself. "I have to find another worker. I can't keep her much longer. Every other week she's calling off. I try, I truly try. One more time and she's gone, that's it".

There's a knock at the door and I see Sarah peek inside. "Miss Aja!!" With a low groin of frustration I look up at her. "Yes, Sarah! How can I help you?" She closes the door behind her and smiles. "There's a customer out there who wants to speak with the owner". "What do they want? And why are you smiling at me like that?" "I don't know what he wants" she said with way too much emphasis on the word he "He just wants to see the owner". "Fine, tell him, whoever he is I'll be there shortly" "Will do!!"

Man, I tell you I can't get any type of work done. Before I walk out I check myself in the mirror. I adjust my facial expression and mentally remind myself to breath and relax my nerves. Once calm I do my sexy check. Yes still looking fab-u-lous.

I expect nothing less of myself. Make you wanna slap your momma cause I'm looking so dam fine. Nothing like a boss lady who got her shit together.

Before you think it, No I'm not stuck up I've just been busting my ass for years. People think this shit comes easy, but it doesn't. You try being raised in the projects with roaches and shit, barely any food, Eating chicken every dam day in all kinds of way, plain chicken, fried chicken, baked chicken etc. with rice for a side.

After so many years seeing my mom busting her butt to make a living for me and my sisters, I refused to put myself through what she went through. Not saying that I don't appreciate everything she did for us because she's a strong woman. I give her all the glory for that. Let's just say if it was me, I wouldn't know what to do, enough about my childhood. Let me get out here and see who needs my service.

Eleven o' clock and the store is already busy. Sarah is at the register cashing out a young lady. I look at her with questioning eyes, she nodes her head towards a gentleman with his back turned to me. I approach as not to startle him. "Hello! I'm the owner, Aja. How can I help you?" He turns to face me "Hello, my name is Todd" and shakes my hand.

Shocked by the view, it takes me a minute to regain my senses. Todd must be in his early 30's, good hair, caramel completion, eyes that remind me of milk chocolate, a mouth that looks like it can work magic. Dam, I need a man so bad that he has me feeling some type of way. Only thought I'm having is sitting on that face to see if he can work wonders. Trying to focus, I clear my throat.

"What can I do for you, Todd?" "I'm an upcoming clothing designer and I'm currently working on some new pieces. I was wondering, if you'd be willing to set up a meeting with me and go over some of my clothing designs. If you're interested maybe you'd be interested in selling them in your store".

Todd just stares at me wide eyed, waiting for an answer. I lick my lips and bite my lower lip dam near salivating at the thought of those lips touching my sensitive spots and that velvet voice asking how I like it? I turn to hide the fact that I'm blushing like a school girl with a crush.

"Well Todd as you can see, all my clothes are made by me". "I've noticed and I must add, you've done a great job. I'm only asking for a meeting and a chance to show off my work and possibly get my feet wet in this industry. I'm sure you would love what I have to offer". "Is that right? How sure are you? I mean do you stand behind your merchandise 100%?" Todd replies with a stern, "Yes, I do!" Normally my first response would have just been a flat out no but I turn to him and say "Ok, give me your business card, I'll look over my schedule and see if I have any time available for a meeting".

Todd says "Thank you! I'm looking forward to meeting with you soon!" "You're welcome, Todd! Have a blessed day!" As Todd walks out the door, he turns around and smiles.

What the hell his smile is even sexy. I release the breath I didn't realize I was holding and wave. Normally, I can handle being around a fine ass man, but this man has me feeling all types of hot and bothered.

I look to see who's around and call Sarah over!! "Yes

Miss Aja". "Next time please take a message. I have work up to my neck to get done" she replies "Ok Miss Aja. He was fine though. Teeth all white and shit. I was about to ask his fine ass if he's in any Colgate commercials with them pearly whites".

I couldn't help but smile at her response. "Sarah, I got to get back to work, you know where to find me". "I'm saying though, Aja! I can see me doing some things with him". Giving Sarah an animated look, I head back to my office and sit at the desk.

Frustrated, tired and now sexually aroused, I'm surprised I didn't cum just listening to him talk. I scold myself. Aja, remember men aren't shit. I got me a dick that I can pick up and pack away, As long as them batteries working we good, Pissed that this man has my hormones on full blast. I start my work….

Fully focused sitting in front on my computer screen Sarah opens the door. "Miss Aja!!" Startled by the sudden interruption I stop typing. "Yes". "Everything is all put away, and money is all counted" "What?"

Looking at my screen I'm shocked "Oh my, look at the time. I can't believe its five o'clock already. Did you put the money in the safe with receipts?" "Yes I did." "Good! Thank you! I'll see you on Monday. Go and enjoy yourself on this beautiful Saturday evening". "Thank you, Aja I will." Sarah leaves out.

Time to shut it down, before leaving I look over the store talking to myself. "Ok! Not bad at all. Everything is clean and neatly put away. She's always on time gets the job done and is always humble. I like that. I might just promote her to manager. I'm going to give it just a little more time before I do that though". Once I'm done talking to myself like a crazy person, I lock up.

As I make my way to my car I can't wait to get home and relax. After the day I've had I need to get my head back together, especially since all my emotions have been tested today after being out last night. Maybe I'll watch a movie and sip on some wine.

Sitting in silence I dam near jump out my seat when my phone rings. I answer, "Hello" "Hey girl what's going on tonight? I was thinking we could go out for some drinks". Even without looking at my caller ID, I automatically recognize that bubbly voice as being my best friend Melissa "Fine, I'll go out for a little bit. The store is closed tomorrow, and I don't have to get up early. Besides I've had a long day and need to unwind. The question is do you have a babysitter?" Leave it to Melissa to be a smart ass with her response. "Of course I got a babysitter, Hell I wouldn't have wasted my breath or time asking if I didn't". "Ok now, relax yourself. I'll be ready by ten".

Melissa is my best friend. To say she's an amazing women would be an understatement. She is a single mother that has three kids, two boys and a girl. Melissa struggled for a bit but is finally getting her shit together. No thanks to that deadbeat daddy of theirs. He left them years ago for another woman. If I ever found myself in her position, I pray I'd have the restraint she has because I know my ass would be in jail.

Shit, I would have put sugar in both of their gas tanks, cut all their tires, and busted out all their fucking windows. Especially after taking everything out the house while I was at work, and the kids were in school. Just thinking about him makes me want to punch him in his throat.

He would have been calling me crazy for sure, because I would have torn him a whole new asshole. I'm so proud of her for being the bigger women in that situation. Anyway, let me get home and get my nap on before we go out tonight. This queen needs her rest for sure.

Chapter Three

The night we meet

"Buzz, buzz, buzz" wakes me with a startled annoyance. I slap the machine into silence. Ugh, I thinking to myself "It's a good thing I set my alarm". Sitting up in bed, I didn't realize how tired I was, I must have knocked out the minute my face hit the pillow. Taking a quick side glance at the alarm clock I see its nine O'clock well I have plenty of time to get my fab-u-lous on.

Just as I'm finishing up my last sexy touch up, my door bell rings. Of course I know it can't be anyone else other than my girl Melissa. I yell "Girl I'm coming, just a minute". I hear her loud bubbly voice echo through the apartment "Hurry up". I grab my keys and purse and open the door. "Took you long enough" she says" Where we going "I ask "To the club of course".

Within minutes we reach Club Magic. The bouncer checks our IDs and we enter. I yell loud enough for her to hear me over the R&B playing "Girl!!! This club is pumping tonight" "Yes honey it is", Melissa replies back as she looks over the crowd. "Aja, do you see that fine ass man over there?"

Searching through the crowd I think I spot who she's referring too. There's a fine chocolate looking brother at the end of the bar, dressed to the T. He looks too be in his late 20's but I could be mistaking. Thinking to myself, there's nothing wrong with getting my grove back. I smirk "Yes, I see him with his chocolate looking ass" make me want to take a bite out of crime "Girl yes! What they saying melts in your mouth and not in your hands."

We both start laughing our asses off. "We so crazy" I say. "No honey, we so horny" she states. I look at Melissa with tears in my eyes from laughing so hard and say "you need not to be horny honey; you might pop out another kid. You know how fertile your ass is. He might touch your face and BAM you might end up pregnant". Toppling over from laughter my cheeks begin to hurt.

"Ha-ha, you got jokes" she says looking at me sideways with a twisted smirk. With one more bout of laughter "No honey I got style" "Lol! You play to much Aja". "I'm sorry do you forgive me with your weak ass self" We both starting laughing again until the handsome chocolate man comes over.

"Excuse me ladies, I couldn't help but notice how nice you both look". In unison we reply "Thank you". Up close I can see he's older then what I expected.

A slight show of salt and pepper to that good hair, light eyes and teeth so white I may need shades on if he keeps smiling. As he reaches out to shake our hands he says "My name is Leon". I sneak a quick glance at Melissa and notice she's got a smile on her face One that obviously says "Hell yes". With a smile I say "Well Leon my name is Aja and this is my best friend Melissa" "Nice to meet you both". "Like wise!" we say in unison again.

Not able to help ourselves we laugh. I'm sure at this point we both feel like yelling Jinx, you owe me a drink as if we were children. Leon turns back to me oblivious to our inside joke. "I couldn't help but notice your smile. It's the kind of smile that would send someone into a dream land".

Thinking to myself, I roll my eyes internally. Here we go with these lame ass lines. I'm going to flow with it though because I'm feeling some type of way. Besides his ass is fine as fuck!!! With a silent huff, I smile "Why thank you, Leon". I spot Melissa giving me the eyebrow raise and jiggle behind him. Dying to crack up I take a sip of my drink and lower my head a bit. "You're so welcome gorgeous. Can I buy both of you a drink?" Melissa and I look at each other, then at him, "Sure, that would be nice, thank you". With a blinding grin he asks, "What are you ladies drinking?" Rum and coke for the both of us please and thank you!" "No problem! I'll be right back".

As he walks away I watch him at the bar ordering our drinks. I know you're thinking this is some stalker type shit the way I'm watching him.

Ladies let me school you right quick. You can't be too careful with people nowadays they might slip something in your drink. Then you'll be all messed up. If you can't see them in your eye sight, then you shouldn't want that drink.

As I continue to watch him at the bar, my eyes burn from not blinking. Yelling to Melissa, "Dam, you see how fineeeee his ass is?" "Girl I seen him. I'm not blind, did you notice how freaking nice he smelled." "Yes girl! I was afraid to open my mouth too much because I was practically salivating, How about them shoes and outfit. Hmmmm, A man that takes care of himself is a beautiful thing. Here he comes".

"Here you go ladies. Rum and Coke for you" he hands Melissa her glass. "Rum and coke for you, Aja" he lightly brushes his thumb over the top of my hand as I reach for my drink. I've be so dam horny lately I could have twitched in pleasure right where I sat. The way he looked at me when he said my name and the warmth of his body radiating so close to mine. My mind and body were reeling.

Melissa must have noticed my discomfort so she says "Thank you, Leon! This was very nice of you". With a quick turn towards her in acknowledgment he says "You're welcome it was my pleasure".

Noticing how Leon moves slightly to the music. I start to wonder how well he moves during other activities. While I'm lost in thought I see Leon turn to me "Aja, would you like to dance?"

Caught off guard by the sudden attention I almost choke on my drink, I take a deep breath and set my drink on the bar. Now that my blood pressure and breathing are back to normal I hear my song playing in the background, I can't pass this up. Quickly so I don't change my mind I say "Sure just one dance".

A triumphant look washes across his face "Ok Beautiful one dance". Turning to my girl I yell "I'll be back, I'm going to dance". Melissa looks at me with a big ass Kool aid smile on her face.

I node as I walk away and think to myself I can't stand her ass sometimes. I wanted to ask "why the fuck you smiling so hard?" But my mind was on getting on the dance floor before my song stopped.

The dance floor was so crowded and hot. There was no way to avoid rubbing up on each other. Which was a little uncomfortable but I just brushed it off. While dancing I couldn't help but notice him looking at my ass.

That's when the voice in my head screamed. Remember men in the clubs aren't shit. The music dies down and a slower beat starts, you know the type, makes you want to bump and grind.

Apparently he forgot about the one dance deal. He wraps his arm around my waist and pulls me closer to him. He leans in close; afraid he's coming in for a kiss I turn my face. He presses his face close to mine and whispers in my ear. "Are you single?" He can't see my facial expression so I roll my eyes thinking, here comes the questions. "Yes I am, why, is there a problem with that? Are you single?" "No problem at all! I'm just saying, you fine as hell, I'm surprised no man has snatched you up yet. Also, to answer your question, yes I am single".

I turn to and give him a look of disbelief. "So you're single, why?" Our dancing pauses for a split second. "Honestly, I'm waiting on the right one". All my alarms go off. He's a player, Aja. Curiosity gets the best of me and I ask anyway. "What's the right one?" "A woman that has her head on right works for herself and has her shit together. That's what turns me on". Dam he's good. Lose for any type of intellectual response. I just say "I hear ya. I feel the same way" No longer in the mood for small talk. We get back into our dance. The music has changed once again so I turn around. All of a sudden his ass gets up on me way to close. I quickly turn back around and say "no, no back up! I don't dance like that unless it's with my man". "I'm sorry I won't do it again. I meant no disrespect".

Incapable of making I coherent remake at that moment, I just node because at that very second, I was saying to myself, "girl did you feel that dick up against your ass like that? That's a big one and he had the nerve to be hard on top of it. Mmmm, the things I can do with that". Here I go thinking crazy, shaking my head. He ask," is everything ok?" I quickly tell a lie. Yes I was just looking at something. He looks at me questioningly "Oh ok!"

Realizing that my mouth suddenly feels like cotton and I'm thirsty as hell, I lean in close to say "I need a drink". Making our way back to my table, I can see my best friend's happy ass smiling like she just seen her favorite R&B singer. I'm 100% sure once we reach the table, this heifer is going to come out the side of her neck with, "you two make a cute couple".

What did I say; do I know this heifer or what?" To make matters worse this man turns around and says "yes we do". That was it for me once he said that shit; I was like "Thank you for the drink and dance. Maybe I'll see you again next time we're out." With a look of confusion he asks "How about you give me your number?" With a sympathetic look I say "I don't think that's a great idea." "Ok no problem". He turns to walk away. Melissa says "Aja"

I pucker my lips and turn to look at her "yes, Melissa". She yells out loud waving her hand towards Leon like a crazy person. "Excuse me; hold on, what's your number? I'll put it in her phone?

Snatching my phone from her I give her the death glare "No you won't". Totally dismissing my look of complete and utter annoyance, she looks at Leon "wait a minute while I talk with my friend, please?" "Sure! He says with a small grin.

Pulling me in close she says "Aja, you don't have a man, hell any life, why are you being so difficult it's just a phone number". Looking at her in shock, like a deer caught in head lights I yell "Excuse me!"

If I wasn't so upset with her at that moment I may have missed it, she looked at me with a subdued look and as quickly as it came it was gone. She readjusted her stance and calmed her tone. "Aja, not like that, I just meant you have no man in your life. I know you're a strong woman who lives by strict rules, but what's life without a little fun now and then. You two make a cute couple. Just talk on the phone, you never know".

With a reluctant node of the head I say "Maybe you're right, but he's in a club, I don't do the club shit." "Girl would you stop, it's just a phone conversation, Maybe a little yum, yum if you're lucky".

Knowing she's right once again and realizing that deep down my best friend feels sad for me I give in "Ok, ok". I walk over to where Leon's waiting. "Leon I'm sorry here's my number give me a call when you're free sometime". He enters my number in his phone "Will do beautiful, thanks for the dance and I'll be in touch. You ladies enjoy your night." Leon walks away and disappears into the crowd. Melissa says "Yes, girl it's about time".

Slowly I turn with my arms crossed over my chest I look straight in her eyes and say, "you ever do that crap again, I'm going to knock you into the middle of next week".

The sound of her laughter was contagious and oddly relaxing. "Maybe now you can get you some real dick instead of that fake one with batteries". My anger subsided as quickly as it came "My fake one does me justice" "Justice my ass, Aja. I'm sure your arms and hands get tired. That's a job. Shit, at least with a man he can flip you, turn you and pound the shit out of you. Make you think you had a V8".

As hard as I tried not to I couldn't help Laughing "Girl, Your crazy" "No honey, you're horny and in need of a real one". Unable to disagree I just answer with "Maybe your right. I'd love to team up with his fine ass and take a bite of crime".

We laughed and continued our night with one drink at a time.

Chapter Four

The morning after

Waking with a massive headache, that felt like drums beating to a tune of heavy metal. I thought "What a fucking hangover". Sitting up, with as little physical effort as possible, I realize I'm still partially dressed from my night out, I make my way to the bathroom and take two Tylenol, splash my face with cool water and look in the mirror. "Holy hell, I look like crap. I can't believe I stayed out till 4am, I'm getting too old for this shit".

Feeling nauseous and weak I check the time "Shit its 2 o click!!" I yell way too loud for my own good. Grabbing my head in pain, I sit on the foot of my bed and cradle my head. Once the crashing waves in my head settle, I head to the kitchen so I can hydrate myself. Gulping down a big glass of water I say "Dam, this taste good as hell" two and a half glasses later, I go back to my room and find some comfy cloths.

Once changed, I Thank God the store is closed today because I really need to get some house cleaning done.

Knowing that my ass is going to be dragging most of the day and I could definitely use about 2 more hours of sleep, I look around and wonder where to begin.

Distracted thoughts of last night replay in my mind as I make my bed. Leon sure seems like he has his shit together, not to mention that nice size dick that rubbed across my ass last night. Had my pussy jumping for joy, like I was about to get some. Maybe Melissa is right about me having strict rules. Maybe I'll let up a little, I mean just a little. Next time though that dam Melissa, better chill, I could kill her, pushing me on Leon like that.

"Ring, ring" my phone vibrates and lights up on my night stand. Moving quicker then I should I grab the phone and hit the volume button, so the noise stops. Looking at the screen I notice the number doesn't look familiar, I wonder who's calling me. I swear people don't let me have a moment to myself, let me see who in the hell is this.

Answering with an attitude I say "Hello"! A smooth silky voice comes threw from the other end of the line "Hello, beautiful"! Recognizing the voice I ask anyway "Who is this?" "This is Leon from Club Magic last night". Trying to dumb down my intelligence a bit I say "Oh hello! How are you?" because obviously I know who he is and where we meet. He replies with "I'm good and yourself?" Feeling the need to say something smart I opt on "I'm a little hung-over, but I'll survive. I didn't think you'd be calling so soon." With a small chuckle he says "Normally, I would have waited but I couldn't get your beautiful smile off my mind". Here he goes trying to smooth talk me with compliments "Is that right?" "Yes, Aja it is. Do you have any plans this evening?" Wanting to knock down his ego just a hair, I wait before answering "Yes I do have plans". When Leon answers back, I noticed his voice changed like a bubble slowly being deflated "That's disappointing, maybe another time then". I can't help but smile "Maybe another time what?" I ask. "Maybe I can take you out to dinner another time since you have plans this evening." he said with a glint of hope behind his voice. Not wanting to sound too eager I waited a few breaths before answering "Well, maybe I can free up some time later. What time were you thinking? I could tell he was smiling when he answered "How about eight? I can come pick you up".

Trying to sound conflicted I say "I may be able to do eight but I'll drive myself". "Is there any place special you would like to go to eat?" he asked. Now I love me some sea food so of course my answer is "How about Red Lobster?"

Waiting to hear that mild huff in his response, you know the one I mean, when a brother wants to get up with you but not actually spend the cash.

With no hesitation he said "That's fine I'll see you at 8 at the main street location". Mildly shocked I said "Ok, I'll see you there!" Just as I was about to say bye and hang up, Leon says " One more thing Aja, don't forget to bring your appetite, I'm not big on salads" Dumbstruck and dare I say slightly turned on, my only response was "okay bye" and I hang up.

Staring at the black screen on my phone, I shake my head and start screaming "I can't believe I'm doing this, I CAN'T BELIEVE I'M DOING THIS". Pacing around my room, my mind hits overdrive. All types of crazy shit start floating around my head, What if he really in a relationship, a killer, or crazy ass person with different personalities. What if he's some type of sexual predator?

I know I'm tripping but that's real though. Trying to focus I wonder, what will I wear? I've got to be on point, searching for an outfit; I realize I still need to do some house work. I guess I'll worry about this in a couple of hours.

Finishing up in the kitchen I turn and look at the clock, its 6:30pm. Dam, time sure flies when you're busy. Taking a quick glance around my apartment, I think good enough, I'm satisfied.

Heading towards my room I hear my phone ringing and think "Now who is calling me?" Snatching my phone off the night stand I look at the number.

Oh wow its Melissa she's not going to believe this shit. I answer, "Hello!! I don't have time to talk I'm getting ready for my date." Wanting to laugh I covered my mouth, because I know this heifer is making her famous 'Awww Shit' face. Just as I expected she stayed silent for too long, with laughter behind her voice she said "Excuse me, your date?" "Yes, girl, I said date. I'm meeting Leon at Red Lobster over on Main Street."

"Well, well look at you miss thing can't talk to your bestie now because you might get some later" she starts to laugh. "You know what; I can't stand your ass. This is all you're doing, so don't be haten now" "Whatever Miss goody to shoe, I'm definitely not haten, you just concern yourself with the things you could be doing later between the sheets" loud bouts of laughter radiated threw the receiver. "Whatever, I don't have time to talk you right now, jerk". "Ok, ok don't get your thongs in a twist; give me a call when you get in. Have fun and be safe!" "I'll try and thank you. Good bye!!"

Setting my phone down, I notice the glowing red numbers on my clock 6:45. Crap, let me hurry up and get in this shower.

Enjoying my nice hot shower I realize I still haven't picked anything out from my closet yet. Thank God I don't have to iron anything. I turn off the invigorating flow of water and grab a towel.

While drying off, I sift through my nicely pressed cloths and decide if I should wear pants or a dress?

Wanting to show off my assets and still look classy, I decide on my royal blue pants that hug my curves perfectly, along with my black and royal blue shirt with my sexy black pumps. Now what am I going to do with my hair? I know I'll put it up in a bun, to show off the welcoming nape of my neck. Talking out loud and Smiling to myself, I say "Yes girl, you gonna look fierce tonight" I mentally high five my dam self. Yes I did that. Either his mouth is going to drop open or he's going to be saying dam to himself.

A quick peak at the clock revels its 7:40pm. I gather my belongings and leave. You never want to be late on a first date. That would be tacky.

As I pull up in my Lexus, I couldn't help but spot him getting out of his Range Rover. Dammmmmmmm, this Negro is fine as HELL and wearing the hell out of that suit.

It was like looking at a slice of mouthwatering chocolate on chocolate cake, you know the one you've been craving for so long, that your mouth starts to salivate before you eat it.

With my heart racing and my hormones on full blast, I turn the engine off and step out the car.

While I cross the parking lot to meet Leon by the door, I notice him raise his eyebrow, take a slow up and down glance of my body and smile. I smiled back 'Oh yes, there's the silent DAM, I was looking for'.

Once I was close enough, he reached over and opened the door. When I walk past I said "Thank you, sir". Smiling with those pearly whites he said "Your very welcome, Aja! You're looking beautiful tonight" Unable to stop my smart mouth I turn too face him and say "Thanks, you're not too bad looking yourself".

Walked into the restaurant was a little unnerving I couldn't help but notice all eyes were on us. You would have thought that we were celebrities or something. Don't get me wrong we definitely make a cute couple, but I'm not thinking that far.

The waitress escorted us to a table at the back of the restaurant. The area was dimly lit and the view from the window was breath taking. Before I could touch my chair, he pulled my seat out for me and made sure I was comfortable before he sat. I took a mental note 'a gentleman'.

Once we were both seated he looked at me and smiled. At that very moment the only thoughts swimming in my mind had nothing to do with real food. I played out the scene in my head.

He comes to stand beside me with a smile and hooded eyes. With a quick sweep of his arm he clears the table. He sets me on the table, leans in close to my ear and whispers. Fuck, I can feel the breeze of his warm breath brush against my ear and neck. I shiver with arousal. He asks "can you be my dinner? Without a word I position myself for easy access so he can taste me, lick me all the way out. I hear myself moan slightly.

"Aja, Is everything ok?" Startled by his attentiveness "Yes, everything's fine" I say with a notable quiver in my voice.

Silently screaming at myself I say "WTF, I have got to get my mind right." Before I could stop myself, he looked at me and my mind checked out again. "Girl, If he don't stop smiling at me like that my pussy going to be all over them lips, making them shiny and wet, like lip gloss!! Before my thoughts continued any further I asked to be excused because if I didn't I would have cum right there.

When I returned to the table it was a relief to find our dinner was served. I couldn't wait to dig in.

I got myself some shrimps and salmon with some broccoli on the side. He orders a lobster tail with a bake potato.

After sitting in silence for what seemed like a life time he asked "Aja, are you enjoying your dinner?" Chewing up the last piece of broccoli in my mouth, I swallow and say "Yes, I am, thank you". "No problem, anytime". I smiled and he hits me with "I can see me with a woman like you. You will compliment me very well. I mean because you have a good head on your shoulders, not to mention you're very beautiful."

Not sure how to respond to that I plaster a smile on my face "Awww thank you, Leon! That's nice of you to say". "You're welcome" he raises his eyes to meet with mine. Trying to relieve some of discomfort I ask "May I ask what is it that you do for a living?" After taking a bite of his potato he set his fork down "Well I'm the owner of, 'Make it your own', I sell houses. Sometimes we flip a property. I found that flipping a property brings in more money, since the value increases".

Completely shocked by this information I swallow "Wow! That's Amazing." Looking at his face I could tell my sudden shock made him happy. He probably assumed I thought he didn't have a good job. He'd be right I just figured he was faking the funk to try and look good.

"What is it that you do, Aja?" "Well, like yourself I own my business and design my own clothing, my business is called Sexy & Classy." His response was "Hmm".

Defensive as usual I looked up at him and thought WTF was that and asked "What do you mean by, hmm?" I could tell he wanted to laugh but instead he looked at me with those smoldering eyes "I'm sorry, I didn't mean anything by it, I just had my own idea of what you did and I'm glad I was right. I can see how design fits you." Not really convinced I said "Thank you".

As the night continued the mood lightened, we got more relaxed, talking and laughing. The conversation and chemistry were flowing smoothly. His smile and laughter were so sincere and infectious as he told me stories. I felt like a crushing teenager.

Surprisingly, I was having a great time and if I was being honest with myself I didn't want it to end but the reality was I had an early morning. Looking at my watch was devastating, just as I had expected it was late and I knew it was time to say good night.

When I looked up at him I know he knew the night

was about to end. I'm sure my face said it all. He stilled and before he could speak another word I said "I'm Sorry, Leon! I have to go; I need to be at work by 7". With a disappointed look he agreed and paid the bill.

Of course while we waited for the waitress to return, my second, now throbbing mind was screaming to be satisfied. NOOOO, don't go I want to fuck him, and let him fuck me GOOD.

Shaking my head mildly I thought WTF is wrong with me, I can't stop thinking like this, for shits sake, I need to get some and soon.

Continuing to be a gentleman he walked me to my car, leaned over and kissed me on my cheek. When he leaned in, I could smell the mix of cologne and his own scent washing over his skin. Inhaling deeply, I felt my heart rate speed and my breath catch. Lord knows I wanted him to kiss me on my lips and I wanted to wrap myself around his hard tone body like a wild animal.

He must have noticed my reaction because he smiled at me with longing eyes, slide his thumb along my cheek and said "Next time...You have a good night, Aja."

Composing myself, not very well mind you, I smiled "You too, Thanks again, it was a nice evening."

"Maybe we can do it again, soon!" "That would be nice, good night, Leon". "Good night, beautiful. I'll call you".

As I watched him get into his truck I drove away thinking he is a breath of fresh air. I can't wait till the next time back to business in the morning.

Chapter Five

At the store

Morning arrived to soon, I got ready and headed out for the day "Good morning everyone! It's nice to see everyone here today. Please make sure at the end of the day that all receipts are in, and that your station is clean". I spotted Tonya but one of the clothing racks "Tonya, can I see you in my office please. Sarah keeps everything on point if you have any problems you know where I'll be."

Heading towards my office I could see beads of sweat forming on Tonya's forehead. Mildly concerned I asked "Is there something going on that I need to know about, Tonya? You've been calling off a lot lately. You have one last call off before I terminate you". Tonya replied back while wiping the sweat off her head. "I've just been really sick". "Do you have a doctor note? Have you seen a doctor?" "No I don't and haven't". Frustrated I turn "Well next time you will need a doctor's note or I will be forced to let you go. Do you understand" Wiping her forehead with her shirt sleeve "Yes Miss Aja, I understand". "I hope so, I'm running a business and if I keep you on it sets a bad example for the rest of the employees. Your lack of attendance is unacceptable. You can go back to work now. Let's make that money!!" With a smile on her face Tonya gets up and returns to work.

Hours have passed when Sarah walks into my office with a vase full of roses and a joker's smile on her face. Confused I ask "Who is this for?" "It's for you, Miss Aja" my eyebrow rose "For me?"

Sarah overly excited wondering who they came from says "Let's read the card, Miss Aja". I purse my lips "How about you go back to work and I'll read my own card miss nosey body." Laughing out loud she turns to leave "ok, I will." "Thank you though!" "You're welcome". As Sarah walks out the door, I grab the card to see who sent me these beautiful red roses. Before opening it I guess who it's from like a high school girl with a sea of boys trying to get a date. I bet Leon sent them.

When I open the card I read Roses are red, violets is blue, guess who wants dinner with you?

What the fuck!!! I read it again thinking my mind was playing tricks. Nope I read it right. "What type of corny shit is this" I said out loud and tossed the card down on my desk.

Now I have a mystery man. Like Come on bro whoever the fuck you are. These lame ass lines be killing me. The roses are beautiful, but those lines got to go. Setting my roses to the side, I start to think of Leon and his fine ass self.

Just the mere thought of him is making me all moist

and shit. I head to the bathroom and wipe myself off so I'm not walking around here all wet.

Please somebody take the wheel. I'm in some serious need of a man's touch. My fake ass dick isn't doing it for me no more. I need a man to throw me on the bed, rip my fucking clothes off and start giving me some head, caressing all my sensitive spots with his warm tongue can't no fake dick do that shit. Returning to my desk I scold myself, Girl get your head back in order.

Starring at my computer screen I try to wrap my head around this crazy email I receive. Startled I jump when my cell phone starts to ring. Not familiar with the number I answer it before it goes to voice mail. I can't express in words how much I hate listening to my messages. Those stupid voice recorded prompts, press 1 to listen, 7 to erase, 9 to save, and if you set a password, awe shit then there's more crap to press, just know the shit is SUPER annoying and a major waste of time and pisses me off.

"Hello" "Oh Hey, Leon! How are you, Movies, Tonight? Mall 7:30? Sure I can do that, see you then". Unable to hide the school girl grin on my face I hang up. This is so exciting; I wasn't expecting to see him again so soon.

Hating to admit it, I had to give my girl Melissa some props, she was right. I needed this and I realize by loosening up on my strict rules a bit, I'm really enjoying myself.

Speaking of Melissa let me give her a call. I'm sure she's mad; I should have called her when I got in last night. She can't fault me though. Hell I was so high off Leon's intoxicating looks and good manners I forgot. Shit I'm surprised I remember my own dam self.

Hesitating before I make my call, I remember why I hate calling her sometimes. It's like being at a crowded concert, yelling at the top of your lungs and losing your voice just to be heard.

That's how our phone calls turn out at least ninety percent of the time. Every time we get on the phone her bad ass kids act the hell up, fighting, yelling and who knows what else. Basically our phone calls consist of me trying to talk as she's hollering at those bad ass kids. After listening to her yell and do nothing, I usually start yelling into the receiver "Girl, if you don't go get the belt and beat their asses".

Yup, this is the number one reason why I don't have or want kids. Screw that, their little asses wouldn't' have me chasing them around like a fool. I'd be the parent waiting for them to attempt a run by with a shoe in hand to throw up side their head, not to hurt then but to slow them down a bit. Sounds horrible right? I'm sure child protective service would be living at my house and they'd get a shoe too of they acted up.

I don't discriminate. Well let me call her real quick, and I mean real quick. Melissa finally answered after about six rings "Hey, girl!! Sorry I didn't call back last night but I was so tired". Here's that 90% I was talking about. As soon as I said "girl, sorry" She started cussing them kids out and they were yelling back "but mom".

First response from me would have been "But mom my ass, go to your room, sit there and count the bubbles on the popcorn ceiling and don't come out till you're done". Yeah I know you're thinking I'm crazy or something.

The truth is kids now a day have no respect for

parents, this entire legal BS saying that we can't whoop our kids or its considered abuse. All children should be disciplined. They need to learn there are consequences for their actions. Now I'm not talking about a whopping so bad that their bruised or injured to the point they need medical attention. I'm talking about a few good swats across the ass with a belt, just enough to sting. This way they think twice before acting like a fool again. Parents are trying to be "friends" with their kids now a day. Fuck being friends, be a parent whoop their asses, teach them respect, consequences, discipline, love and understanding. Don't reward them for bad behavior. They have enough quote on quote friends. Again, this is why I can't be a parent. I don't believe in all this new age parenting shit.

Melissa was so busy hollering. I didn't even attempt to talk about my dinner date. Annoyed I said "girl call me later when you get your kids to bed". Hanging up quickly, I put my face in my hands and took a big woosah breath.

According to my computer screen there's only two hours left before we close, I check my list and get back to work.

Tonya knocked on my door, "Miss Aja, everything is done, we're about to leave". Apparently I was really focused because she actually scared me a little. "Oh, ok, thank you! Have a good night". I watch as Tonya and Sarah leave.

Shutting down my computer and locking up as I leave, my excitement shifts into overdrive. I can't get home fast enough and get ready for my date. Truth be told I can't wait to see his fine ass self.

Chapter Six

The night that changed everything

Turning in to the parking lot I approach the entrance and spot Leon standing by the door looking like an appetizing chocolate bar, wrapped up in an enticing package, all ready for me to gobble up and eat. There's no denying that man can dress his ass off.

Once parked I give myself a once over in the mirror, Still looking fabulous, I made my way to meet him. I lowered my face and took a deep breath before reaching him. I was trying to hide the fact that I was smiling all extra hard and shit while I walked in his direction.

Once I was in hearing distance I spoke "Hello! How are you? Are you ready to go in? Smiling at me with those Pearly whites he says "I sure am beautiful".

We'd been walking around for just a short while, but you could see different women staring at him and whispering to each other. Dam I forgot how women are like vipers ready to strike at any moment. Jealousy and claim took over. In my head I was yelling at those bitches to "stop looking at my man". I'm not entirely sure why but I was really feeling some type of way. I'm sure he noticed all eyes on him but he kept looking straight. It was like none of those women existed. Treading unfamiliar territory in my mind, I wondered if I wanted him to be my man. I visibly smiled because even in my head that shit sounded funny. Man! Ha what a laugh.

Once we got our tickets we headed to the concession stand. I ordered popcorn and water he got pretzel bites and sprite. In the theater we decided to sit in the very back furthest from the screen. Since it was his idea to come to the movies he picked "The Nun". I'm sure he picked a scary movie so I'd be jumping all over him and shit. Not like I wouldn't like it.

Just as the lights dimmed low and the movie started, he placed his hand on top of mine. Lord knows I didn't need a man touching any part of my body because my body was talking all types of shit.

Ahhhhhhh, screaming out loud I put my face right into his arms. He was laughing his ass off, whispering I got you baby; I won't let anyone hurt you. Of course I kept my smart mouth shut, because all I wanted to say was you need to stop trying to be all extra like you getting some tonight.

When the movie ended he held my hand as we left. I was still shaken up because I hate scary movies and that movie was scary.

Just When I thought this was going to be good bye for the night he asked if I would mind having a drink with him at his house.

Holding back a grin I nicely replied "back to your

house?" "Yes beautiful, my house. I mean I know we don't know each other all like that yet, but you might try to take advantage of me." He started laughing and said "Don't worry your fine and all that, but not that fine for me to go to jail for some bull shit like what you might be thinking. I have too much going on, to lose everything behind some craziness".

Before answering I thought to myself, He's right and talks a good game but some men don't care about anything. They just want what they want regardless. Ignoring all the sirens going off in my head I say "I guess, I can stop by for a little bit, I'll just follow you". "Cool" he said. He proceeded to walk to his truck after making sure I was in my car.

About fifteen minutes later we pulled into his driveway. I met him at his car looking around at the amazing view. "Wow, Leon! This is his house? It's so beautiful. I can't wait to see what the inside look like." He smiled and took me by the hand and we walked up the stairs leading to the glass double doors. My jaw dropped once we entered his house, holy shit this place is beautiful!

This man really has it going on. I followed him into the large kitchen which was fashioned with red, black, and white. So elegant and romantic, puts you right into a good mood. I always felt those colors went well together.

I seated myself at the large White and black marble top island that was positioned perfectly in the middle of the kitchen. I made quick notice of the room as he poured us both a glass of rum and coke. When I took a sip I couldn't help but say, "So you remember what I was drinking the night you met me, Very impressive".

Leon eyed me as he took a long gulp of his drink. I felt my body warming up. "How can a man forget that? If he forgets the little things, he will never remember the big things. If he remembers the big things and not the little things, well he's a man that just wants to play games. I look at it like this, a real man going to make sure whoever his lady is that she's going to be ok, especially if he is in love with her. A person can tell you that they love you, but if their actions speaking something else, then they just using the word to string that person along."

I couldn't help but smile at the way he was talking; he sure was saying all the right things.

While still making small talk he took me into his living room and we sat in front of the fireplace on his oversized fluffy carpet.

Feeling slightly uncomfortable with the way he was just looking me up and down, like a hunter with his prey. I sipped my drink and asked him if there something wrong? "Not really. The only thing wrong is the fact that I haven't kissed you yet." Ahhh shit I couldn't help but smile or help that fact that my body temp just went up a few degrees. Trying to stay composed I looked him straight in the eyes, licked my lips and bit softly at my bottom lip and said "is that right?" "Yes that's right" he leaned in closer and practically whispered "Aja, do you mind if I kiss you?"

My body ignited with excitement and screamed yes, yes kiss me, touch me, carry my ass into the next room and fuck the shit out me you fine piece of chocolate, Taking a deep breath to control the sudden outburst of internal sexual excitement. I slowly leaned into his gesture and said "no I don't mind".

Shifting his body he slid his hand up my arm and placed it on the nap of my neck. I watched as he slowly moistened his lips before leaning in the last few inches. Gently his lips caressed mine like a warm breeze flowing off the ocean caressing my body. You know the kind that causes goose bumps. A low moan escaped my mouth as his soft warm tongue parted my lips and entered my mouth. Slowly the eagerness of the kiss began to change as we found our dance. My hormones kicked into overdrive wanting to feel the warmth of his body next to mine. I moved my body closer to him and heard a low growl come from the back of his throat. At the sound of this my inner good girl screamed "Girl, slow down and chill".

Slowly I eased up and began to pull back from his lips but once I looked into his smoldering eyes, I couldn't help but lean back in for another kiss. This time he held my face with a hand on each side.

Sirens and flashing signs that read "Danger, Danger" played in my head. My inner good girl lost all her will power. She screamed "Bitch it's about to go down. No fake dick tonight" hell she may have even done back flips, he gently laid me down on my back closer to the fireplace so I could feel the warmth of the flames brushing your skin.

His passionate kiss ignited every molecule in my body causing a low buzz from my head to my toes. While making his way down my neck with soft butterfly kisses he slowly slid his hands up and down the outside of my thick ass thighs. Eventually I felt a warm finger rub my waste and he looked at me for approval. With only a deep breath as a response, he slowly slid his hands under my shirt being mindful to caress every inch of me before he slid my shirt off.

Looking at my almost naked flesh he smiled and moaned. I'm so fucking glad I wore my sexy lingerie. His kisses traveled to the top of my full breast, taking his fingers he slowly slide my bra straps from my shoulders releasing my breast from their confinement. My nipples were puckered up and waiting for his touch. He suckled my nipples, and with his warm tongue he slowly licked around my nipple as if he was licking ice cream up from the side of a cone.

This man had my ass so turned on, horny and wet. He licked and kissed down my stomach and then took his tongue and ran it just under the waste if my pants, like an animal taste the air with his tongue. My clitoris started jumping for joy and I couldn't help but moan with excitement.

Picking up on how bad I wanted his face between my legs he returned to my breast and mouth. I didn't mind because he felt so good and his big fat dick was hard as hell. The anticipation made this sexy and adventurous. Little did he realize the longer be played the more it turned me on. My pussy and panties were getting wet as hell. Kissing me on my neck sucking on my nipples I could hear his breathing pattern change. I felt his fingers work the button on my pants and heard the zipper being undone. My inner sex goddess was screaming "YEESSS" as he kissed all the way down to my belly button; he slowly slid my pants down to my ankles and pulled them off.

Leon sat on his knees for a moment staring at me with hunger and want. I felt my toes curl with the shear intensity. He stood and began to remove his cloths. Standing there in nothing but his boxes I was in awe of how truly fucking sexy this man was.

He lowered himself to his knees and grabbed my foot and lifted my leg. With a grin he turned to me and said "you have no idea how sexy you are". Lightly his kisses started from my toes, up my calf then in between my thighs. He made sure to include my other leg but this time the pot of gold was about to be tended to. I felt the warmth of his breath close to my pussy and his tongue lick over my moist goodness. He used his teeth to move my panties to the side and held it with his finger. He slowly started kissing and licking and sucking my pussy.

Slowly I began grinding my hips with the movements of his mouth. I started moaning and groaning, saying "this shit feels so fucking good, you're about to make me cum". His sucking and licking began to quicken with such intensity that it was almost hard to breath. Threw my loud moans I heard him say "cum in my mouth baby cum, I want you to feel good. Let me taste your loving". Once he said that, I came so hard in his mouth that he had all my loving around his lips.

While I was breathing heavy he said "Good girl" and swallowed, took a breath and said "Dam baby you taste so fucking good. Look at how hard you got my dick." The sight of his hard erect dick made me shutter like electricity had coursed through my veins. Shit that dick looks good and ready.

After wiping his lips off completely, he made his way up my body one kiss at a time, finally he made it to my mouth and began to kiss me.

Some might say that's nasty and I'd reply with No the hell it's not! I'm clean and I stand behind my product 100%. What the fuck y'all think.

Leon continued Kissing, sucking, and nibbling my lips. In reaction every part of my body was tingling and twitching with excitement. I'm 100 % sure he knew exactly what he was doing to me. I could almost feel his grin threw my closed eyes and our locked lips.

Feeling his big fat dick rubbing against my pussy, I knew without a shadow of doubt he was about to tear my ass up and FUCK yes I was ready for it.

Slowly he began to position himself for better access. I could feel the head of his dick toying with me. Around and around it teased at the entrance of my warm, moist pussy.

Fuck, he's killing me. My pussy was throbbing with want. I'm sure we've all played this game before. You know the teasing game, give a little, take away a little, and leave them at the point of begging for it.

I have no shame in begging and at this point I was about to wrap my legs around his rock solid body and force him to enter my goodness. That's when I felt it and my breath hitched.

Slowly his fat dick started to penetrate my slick pussy. Unable to contain my thoughts I yelled out loud "fuck you got a big dick". With only the head of his penis inside me he leaned over and whispered in my ear, "don't worry baby, I'll be gentle with you". He slowly started stroking the walls of my pussy. In, out, in out until he was able to fit his entire dick inside me.

Leon was hitting all types of shit inside my pussy.

Again and again he entered me deeper and deeper making sure to take his time.

I laid there moving my hips in sync with his every thrust. Clutching the rug under my body I could feel my climax coming again. I screamed out loud "Dam you feel so good, you about to make me cum again".

No faster then I say that, he pulled out and started sucking my pussy again until I came with a blood curdling moan.

My body convulsed when he rubbed my clit with his thumb and he smiled. In one swift move he had me on my hands and knees. Rubbing my ass, he moaned or should I say growled in the back of his throat.

Wrapping his hands around my waist I felt him pull me back slightly. Even though I knew what was about to happen it still shocked me. That's when I felt it, all 12 inches of his big fat dick pounding the shit out of me.

In my head I was like "dam Negro slow down your dick about to come out of my belly button", that's how far he was up in me.

Again with a swift movement he had me on my back with my legs up and over his shoulders. Shit, I could really feel his dick now.

Still grabbing me by my waist he pounded into me quickly, slowly, quickly, slowly and again and again. His face was sweaty and his features alive with bliss. This is the moment my climax struck again and my rational mind intervened with "FUCK I forgot about a condom". As quickly as the thought entered my mind it was gone.

My body betrayed me when spurts of electrical like

jolts coursed through my body. I came hard again and again losing all control and concern.

He slowed down his thrusts, brought my legs down and wrapped them around his waist. Slowly penetrating me in and out, pausing long enough to watch my reaction every few strokes.

I tightened my pussy all around his dick, and thrust my hips up to meet his moves, allowing all of him to enter me. He was so deep in me that I could feel my pussy rub against his waste.

Speaking out loud he said "Shit, baby this pussy is so good and wet". Within seconds he let out this growl like he was a lion or something. Quickly he pulled out and came all over my stomach.

It looked to me like I wasn't the only one in need of some loving. It was like a gallon of milk just spilled on my stomach. He stood up and went to get me a towel so I could wipe my stomach off.

Sitting up to gather my cloths I glanced at the clock. Shit its 2am. Without hesitation I started to dress.

Leon just watched as I moved in a rush to get dressed. Pausing for but a moment, I looked at his flawless face and said "I got to go; I have to get up in a couple of hours for work".

With understanding in his eyes he quietly said," I wish you could stay, maybe next time?" feeling a little enthusiastic by his response I said "Yes maybe next time. I need to get home and shower. I truly thank you for tonight. I had a great time with you".

Before reaching the door Leon gave me a gentle kiss me on the side of my cheek and told me to call him once

I got home so that he knew I made it safe. "Will do talk to you soon" I stepped away from the house.

Walking to my car with a little pep in my step, I got in the driver's seat and noticed him watching out the window.

I think, "Wow, A man that cares, has a great conversation and good dick, not to mention he knows how to eat pussy and I mean REALLY eat pussy, plus has his shit together. What more could a woman ask for.

Subconsciously my sensible mind snuck in like a predator in wait for his unknowing prey "Girl, you know it's too good to be true". Ugh I hate my rational side, Right now though that shrewd bitch is not about to screw with my happy reckless behavior.

Finally home, I hit the shower and take my ass to sleep. I'm so tired.

CHAPTER SEVEN

Nothing but smiles

Beep, beep, beep.... With an outstretched arm I silence the alarm with a quick tap on the top of the clock; with every bit of effort I could muster up I turned my head to look at the time.

Instead of focusing on the near future "" work "" I decide to reminisce about last night. The very thought of this man has me smiling from ear to ear, like a child on Christmas morning receiving the most important gift on his or her wish list.

Sliding on my slippers I attempt to make my way to the bathroom. If you missed the key word in that sentence it was ATTEMPT.

WTF, Holding my pussy and let me NOT forget to mention walking funny; I finally reached the bathroom with some serious effect I must add. Dam, That man's dick is so big that my pussy hurts.

There's no question about it I need to soak my ass in

the tub for about a half an hour. Maybe it will ease the pain some.

Getting to work later than expected, I notice everyone stop and stare at me, Feeling uncomfortable due to the sudden scrutinizing look of my employees, I look at them and ask "what the hell are you all staring at? Can't I be late once?" I failed to mention the reason for tardiness was I needed a full hour of tub time.

Sarah was first to respond," you Miss Aja. You have this smile on your face and a glow about you this morning. Is there any chance you got some last night?"

Struggling to keep a poker face I turn to her and say," Ha that's none of your dam business and if I did in which I didn't, I would have gave all of you the day off" a small giggle escaped the back of my throat! "That was a joke now back to work please and thank you. Sarah you know where I'll be, if you need me". "Ok Miss Aja.

Once I got myself all settled, guess who walked in my door, Melissa. "What you doing here?" I said maybe a little harsher then I'd like.

"I was in the neighbor and I just wanted to stop by to see my best friend." She scrutinized my face as she sat in the chair opposite from me. "Wait a fucking minute. Is that a glow I see on you?" With a smile I kindly said, "No bitch". She smiled "Aja you fucked him didn't you?"

I hadn't realized my office door was open until Sarah walked passed and glanced at me. I'm sure she heard Melissa's big mouth. Calmly I stood up walked to my office door and closed it.

With my poker face now gone I turned to Melissa and

began to jump up and down and yell “yes bitch, yes and the dick was so good”.

Laughing like school girls we sat down to talk. “I knew it. Your smiling and shit with a glow.” “Melissa it was amazing, girl he’s like a dream come true.”

Skeptical she looked at me “Aaaa, now hold your horses, don’t go moving all fast and shit. Yes your ass needed some dick, but don’t go crazy”.

Waving my hand at her, “Girl please I just want to have some fun that’s it. He’s not my man or anything like that.” A little annoyed I stand and walk to the window. “Wait a minute weren’t you the one who told me to ease up? It’s just a phone number; maybe some yum, yum and shit like that?”

With a stunned look she says “Yes, that’s exactly what I said for some dick and fun. Not to go deep in so fast.”

“Well excuse me! I’m doing what you said having fun. Is that ok with you? Now who sounds responsible?” “Yes its fine, just take your time with him, Hell fuck him as much as you can. He’s got you smiling and walking funny and Shit. It must be good”

With my eyes wide and mouth covered I start laughing. Lowering my hand I whisper “Is it that obvious, that you can you tell?” To this my ass of a friend starts to laugh so hard that a tears slip from the edges of her eyes. “Yes! I can tell. Did you really think it would go unnoticed that you’re moving a little off. That Dick must be big as hell.”

Slightly embarrassed because I really thought I was looking good. I guess not “Girl yes it is fucking big.”

“Dam bitch I’m feeling a little jealous. NOT. Get that shit in girl and you better learn how to handle it. You can't keep walking around like someone kicked you in the crotch."

Laughing I say "Girl get out my store I got work to do." Ok! We'll talk later. We hug and say I love you like always. She truly is like my sister. Once I was alone again I stood in the mirror to practice my walk. I don't need any one else noticing my funny walking ass from that big fat dick. After about fifteen minutes I felt more comfortable with my walk and get back to work.

Trying to get my work done I find I'm unable to concentrate. Hell I can't even type a full sentence without my mind wandering back to last night. Smiling, I pick my phone up and look at his number. You know what I'm just going to call him.

The phone just rang and just as I was about to hang up I heard "Hey there! How are you?" Happier than I'd like to admit I said "Good! I was just thinking about you and wanted to say hi."

Listening to the sound of his voice soothed my unsettled nerves. "Tonight and you're cooking? What can you cook, Hot dog and beans?"

He laughed at my smart remark which was unexpected. I figured he'd be offended somehow. Without a pause in his conversation he set a time. "No problem I'll see you at 8. Have a good day".

After hanging up the phone my pussy started jumping again. I can't believe this shit. Even more concerning was the fact that I started to talk to her "Bitch, he already fuck your ass up last night. His dick has me walking all funny and shit. You better chill out literally. Hell I need to get home and sit your ass on some ice before tonight." Cracking myself up I continue with my work.

Lord knows this man has got it going on and I can't wait to see him tonight.

After some serious concentration on my part I was able to wrap things up for the day. Just when I thought I could pack up and leave there was a knock at the door. Slowly the door opened and Sarah looked in, "Miss Aja that man from last week is here to see you."

I'm sure the look on my face said way more than my response "What man Sarah?" "Todd!!"

Cupping my face and inhaling a deep breath I looked up at Sarah "You know what send him in please and thank you."

Todd stood in the door way like a statue and said "Hello". "Come in, Todd" I stood up to grab his out stretched hand for a shake. I noticed his hand was sweaty. Obviously he must be nervous

"Nice to see you again, how are you?" "I'm doing well, Todd. How can I help you, today?" "Well I know I'm coming off as a little eager but I was waiting for a phone call, but I hadn't received it yet, so I figured I'd stop back in and try my luck."

"I apologize I've been very busy. What did you want to speak to me about?" "If you recall I mentioned that I design clothing. I truly believe my clothing designs would do well here and there appropriate for your store title Classy & Sexy.""

Watching his eyes light up as he spoke about his clothing, I was definitely impressed by his confidence.

"Is that right? Do you have anything with you now?"

His enthusiasm was addictive. Heck, he got me excited to see what his clothing looked like. I just hope he's as good as he thinks he is, I'd hate to have to crush his fine ass. Reaching over to grab his bag, his excitement was palpable. "Of course, yes I do" as he handed me his portfolio.

I slowly turn through the pages making sure to keep a poker face, just in case his drawings are trash. Lord knows I've been told many times that my face speaks my thoughts before my mouth. Once I was done I lifted my face to look at him and cleared my throat. He was staring so hard at me that he could have burnt a hole in my face.

Before I could speak he leaned in close and said "Well, what do you think?" I stayed silent for longer than need be but I just wanted to screw with him. "Well, Todd. I definitely see your potential" pausing again for effect I looked him in the eyes and laughed.

"Oh" he said. The shock and despairing look on his face made me feel like a complete. I was not my intention to make him feel bad.

This time when I spoke I didn't hesitate "I'd like to discuss your future here at Classy & Sexy in further detail unfortunately, my time is limited today, Are you available next week Thursday lets say1pm?"

"Are you serious?" His expression was so priceless I would have loved to capture the moment on my camera. "Very! I find your work to be impressive, very tasteful, classy and sexy. Let's just say you're a very talented man, Todd and I'm not easily impressed.

The atmosphere in my office was so thick with contentment and exuberance or any other word you'd like to use for happiness, the feeling was tangible. I could feel it wrap around me like a soft blanket on a cool night soothing me to the core.

Delighted he shook my hand "Thank you, Aja! Thank you so much". "You're welcome; I'll see you next Thursday. Have a good day". As he walked away I heard him say "I'm having a great day.

I watched as he left thinking dam, that man is fine as wine, but my thoughts turn back on, Leon. It's only been a couple weeks but he's already got me feeling like a kid in the candy store.

With a smile on my face I focus on our date tonight. I wonder what he's cooking. Hopefully he can taste my pussy again. That man sure knows how to please a woman.

Here goes my pussy jumping again. Hell l would jump to if someone was licking me like that. LMAO!

Someone please help me. My sexual emotions are out of control, Lol!

Without another thought I grab my belongings and leave.

I can't wait much longer to go get fucked, I mean sucked, hell all of it.

Chapter Eight

The right things to say

The drive home felt like a life time, maybe because I was egger as fuck to go get my groove on. I need to get right so I make a quick stop to freshen up and change my cloths. Ten minutes later I'm fresh and fine and out the door.

Arriving at his house in record time I knock and I could hear a low voice say "come in".

Opening the door my senses are washed over with the smell of sea food and spices he must be in the kitchen, I thought. Yelling into the obis "Wow babe it smells so good in here." Again in a low voice he said "Thank you! I made some shrimp and Lobster tail with broccoli and yellow rice".

Entering the hallway leading to the kitchen the view was arousing. A fine ass man working his magic, delicious aromas swam in the air, the vibrant colors of vegetables were enticing and let's be real he was the only main course I was looking forward to.

Standing in the door way I watched in awe "DAM!! You give it up like that?" "Only for you babe" He looked up at me with a smile and winked then continued doing his thing.

Since I have no filter on my mouth, I responded with "Are you part of the main course?" He laughed and proceeded to pour me a glass of wine.

Bringing me the glass he said "You know I could be the main course and you my dessert every night if you just be my Queen".

For the first time ever I was lost for words, although my face probably showed a few that were unspoken. His face was hard to read though. Was he serious? After an awkward amount of silence the only coherent words that came out were "your queen". "Yes, my queen". "Are you asking", before I could finish my sentence he leaned in and kissed me.

Holding my chin in his hand he starred in my eyes. "Yes, I'm asking you to be my lady".

WTF, my mind turned to jelly. All intellect seemed to disappear. I wasn't sure how to react. So I stuck to the facts "We've only been seeing each other for two weeks. Don't you think we're moving too fast?"

"Maybe a little but I want you to be all mine. Don't you want the same?"

Having no response at that moment he acted like I had answered and proceeded to take my hand and sit me at the table. He placed a plate of food in front in me and did the same for himself.

Unnerved by his nonchalant display I finally responded "Well, I do, but I don't, I'm conflicted." He shoveled a spoonful of food in his mouth and waited for me to explain. Taking a deep breath I continued "Leon, look I just don't want to get hurt from moving too fast. I mean I've had my share of hurts. I'm not in the mood for BS anymore."

As he sat across from me and starred, He poked the fork into a shrimp on my plate and placed it in my mouth slowly. Reaching over to place his hand on mine he said, "Babe! Not all men come to play games. I came to restore and rebuild. I want someone that I can give my all to. I don't want to half step. I want to take the right steps. The way you and I have been connecting, I feel in my heart that you're the one. You have your own business; you have a good head on your shoulder. Did I mention how fine you are?"

"Yes, you did. I understand how you feel. However, I need to know that you won't run when things get ruff. Some men can't handle the pressure of real situations. When the heat gets going, y'all run into the arms of another woman thinking that grass is greener on the other side but once you've realized it's not, y'all want to run back to the previous relationship. I can't deal with those types of games anymore."

As he was still placing food in my mouth, he replied with, "Baby only God knows my Heart and you just have to trust in him and allow us to live and enjoy one another".

Shocked by his response I wasn't sure how to react. I'm sure my facial expression spoke a thousand words like "no he didn't put God in this, and what does he know about God anyway".

Silence consumed the air around us the only noise was

the swirling thoughts in my head. "He sure knows exactly what to say, he's smart as hell too and let's not forget he has it going on but something just don't feel right".

As if sensing my internal battle He turned to me grabbed my hand and looked at me with those smoldering eyes and asked again "Aja, would you be my lady?" I found myself lost in his eyes and that bright beautiful smile splayed across his face made me feel all warm and fuzzy inside.

Against all of my internal warning signs I couldn't help but say yes. Shame on me I thought I just went against everything I've preached to my friends and myself.

Overjoyed with my answer he started hugging me, kissing me and hell he even spun me. "Thank you. I promise I'll do my best to keep you happy".

Looking at me with sultry eyes he took me by the hands pulled me close. Slowly and passionately he began to kiss me. I felt my knees begin to weaken so I leaned against the sink as I continued to enjoy the moment.

Playfully he began to lick and kiss the nape of my neck. All of my senses were aroused once I felt his hand began to caress the skin under my shirt. His warm, soft hands made it to my full and perky breast and slowly he rubbed and played with my nipples to point that they were hard as hell.

Sensing my excitement he moved his hand slowly and intentionally down my waist to my thigh, I softly gasped when he slide his hand under my skirt and rubbed my pussy. I felt his smile across my lips when he moved my panties to the side and gently rubbed my pussy slow and with purpose.

Getting me all kind of wet, like I'm sure he intended, he knelt down and began to taste my pussy. No words can truly explain the feelings that course through my body when this man touches me the way he does. Biting on my bottom lip I hold back a moan, I can feel myself about to cum from him tasting me, It feels so good.

Over whelmed by the need to cum, I placed my hands on the back of his head to pull him in closer to my pussy. Slowly I began to grind on his face while his tongue licked and sucked my pussy.

I shit you not it was so dam good I could almost feel my clitoris swell with excitement, with a stunted breath I screamed out loud

"I'M CUMMING!!"

While gathering my breath, Leon stood up and smiled. At that very moment my body began to sing. Yes I said sing not like a song but with an over whelming sense of joy because I knew that the smile he gave me meant that shit was about to go down.

Just as I expected he turned me around and bent me over the kitchen sink, slowly he raised my skirt to my waste and slides his big fat dick inside me.

Gently he started moving his dick in and out of my wet pussy. While I enjoyed the feel of him filling me I heard him say "Mmmm, dam baby your pussy is so fucking good, you creaming my dick the fuck up."

After that comment gentle flew right out the window. I began to grin with his movements as he started pumping in and out real fast. Placing one of his hands on my ass cheek to lift it up some more he said "Fuck Shit, give me that pussy baby, give it to me, this my pussy, take this dick."

At that moment it was true my pussy was officially his. Screaming out loud, I said "this is your pussy daddy. Shit! You're fucking my pussy up." Pumping faster "Dam right I am, this is mine!! Oh fuck I'm about to cum babe." With one last pump in I felt him pull back and Next thing you know I had cum dripping all down my legs. Hot, sweaty and breathless we stood in silence for a moment. This is the moment I truly believed that he meant it when he said "I promise I'll do my best to keep you happy".

Once we gathered our breath I said "Babe I need to take a shower after all of that." "Hell me too" he said looking me up and down. "Come on then let's go take a shower" I said.

Once we were in the shower, rinsing under the running water he began rubbing his dick against my ass, getting all hard again. I turned to look back at him and asked "you're not tired?"

Again with that smile He was like "hell no. I need some more of that sweetness."

Shocked for a moment in my mind I was like shit this Negro can fuck. Most men need a reboot time, apparently not him.

Placing both my hands against the wall he lifts both my ass cheeks up and slowly places his dick back in me. As the water falls on the both of us, the bathroom becomes hot and steamy. The feel of him and the temperature in the room are breath taking. He was fucking me all so well.

As he stroked my insides I thought to myself "I'm going to have to start sucking this man dick. He isn't going to keep having me walking around funny and shit. Fuck, he's trying to have his dick go through my belly button and shit. That's how deep his ass feels."

Could you imagine going to the hospital for that and they ask you what happened? And having to say "Dick happen a big fat dick."

Without realizing it I laughed a little out loud. Right away he was like "you laughing at me babe." Caught off guard I said "No babe I'm not." "I think you are." He grabbed my waste pulling me close to him and started fucking the shit out of me till he came. I finished washing up and got out of the shower. Once dry and dressed I laid down in the bed with heavy eyes and an extremely joyful hoo-ha. I don't think I've ever been so happy to lie down. Shortly after he settled in next to me and we laid in silence for a few minutes when I rolled over to face him "Thank you baby! That was so wonderful. I'm so happy that you're all mine." Rubbing his fingers up and down my arm he looked me in the eyes and said "Me too babe" Thinking how sweet in that moment he continued with "Do you think we could do it one more time before we go to sleep."

HELL NO! I jump up and looked at him. His face was priceless a look of surprise and seriousness. He really wanted to fuck again.

"You know what I'm going to do. I'm going to learn how to suck your dick. You're not going to keep beating up my walls."

Laughing out loud, he pulls his dick out and says "I can teach you right now. Just kiss it for me." Still shocked by how big his dick is I say "Ha how about you kiss that pillow and go to sleep." "So you're going to leave me like this?" "Dude have you seen your Dick? That shit will stretch my mouth into different shapes. What the fuck! You already have me walking funny, now you want my mouth to be shaped funny as well." With uncontrollable laughter he looks at his dick "Your funny babe. Just kiss the top of the head for me and I'll go to sleep" "Negro!" "PLEASE" Those Fucking eyes "ok just one little kiss." As I put my face down to kiss it he says "now put the whole thing in your mouth." I jump up, give him a jerk look and say Good night!" Unable to help himself he lets out a full belly laugh "I was just kidding babe. Good night!"

Chapter Nine

Six months later

Six months have passed and we're so in love, I would I have never thought that we would move in together but when you know, you know. Yes, I know it was a shock to me too, especially since everything was going great. So much so I couldn't help but just say fuck it and enjoy the ride and let me tell you what a great ride it has been," pun intended", LOL.

Surprising myself I moved into his house. If you haven't noticed I've always been the independent type, due for myself and have my own. He really did chip away at my walls, making me feel real secure with him.

The way his eyes seem to brighten when he looks at me and the way his kisses and touch, just make my heart melt. If Melissa would have told me six months ago that I'd be involved with someone from the club, I would have called her crazy. Leon, was just meant to be a toss in the hay, you know an "Aja, got her groove back" kind of thing.

Sometimes I have to pinch myself to see if I'm

dreaming, this situation is so new and foreign to me, Ouch, Nope I'm not!! Dam I really do love this man.

Sitting there daydreaming about the love of my life, I'm startled to awareness by the slamming of the front door.

BANG!! Jumping up I make my way to the front entrance. Leon was pacing back and forth in a fit of furry; I could tell this man was mad as hell.

Concerned and not quite sure how to approach him, as calmly as I could I asked "What's going on babe? Is everything alright?" Mind you I've never seen him this pissed and to be honest I was a little nervous.

He replied with such anger and such venom in his voice that I found myself taking a step back. "HELL NO! They took my business license away. Claiming I didn't have certification for certain equipment I used. So no babe everything is not alright. Those people are always fucking with me".

Cautiously I Step forward and place my hand on his arm "I'm sorry to hear that babe. How can we fix this?"

"I don't fucking know. I have to wait on some paper work or a court hearing. This is some fucking bullshit. How and I suppose to pay my employees and my house if I can't work without a license?"

"Well, don't you have some money put away for an emergency?" his response was so loud that it echoed of the hall walls. "DON'T YOU THINK I HAVE SOME? THAT'S JUST SOME, FOR HOW LONG I DON'T KNOW".

'Well I can help as much as I can. Don't worry we got this", "Yeah Yeah! So you say".

Now a little pissed because he's being shitty towards me I say "No so I know. Look I understand that you're upset but there's no need to take it out on me. We can figure it out until your license is fixed. I'm going to fix you a drink so you calm down some".

Staring at me with slits as eyes he said "A drink would be good right about now. In fact how about some pussy I need to bust a nut".

With a look of horror on my face my only response was "Excuse you!!" "You heard me. All this bullshit got me extra hard". Flabbergasted by what is going on I say "I don't feel like it" and began to walk away.

I could hear his footsteps behind me "What the fuck you mean you don't feel like it?" "I have a headache." He snatched my arm and turned me so now I was facing him. His eyes looked black and his anger was radiating off him like steam as he held on to me. "Bitch, if you don't get your ass over here and pull them pants over and bend that ass over, we going to have some fucking problems." "What the hell, Leon! Why are you talking to me like this?" "I'm not asking again, Aja! Pull those pants to the side". His fingers were squeezing my arm so hard that I felt tears in my eyes. "Leon, you're hurting. Please let go. I know you're having a bad day. Why don't you just go and take a nap, I'll fix dinner."

Turning me so that my back was now facing him he pushed my body up against the kitchen table. "Since you won't bend that ass over, I'm going to bend it over for you", tears now running down my face, I could hear him unzipping his pants. I've never seen him like this before. Forcefully he pulled up my skirt and ripped my underwear off and rammed his dick in me. You would have thought someone lite a flame under his ass. He was thrusting so fast and hard that He was hurting me. I couldn't stay quite so I yelled out loud "slow down, you're hurting me".

He said, "Shut the fuck up and take it like a woman and stop being so fucking weak. You should be used to this dick by now. If you can't handle this dick, I'll get someone that can".

Tears just poured from my face like rain. I couldn't believe what this Negro was saying to me. I was hurt and hurting from the way he was fucking me. My screams came out like tidal waves, fast and furious, the pain was unbearable.

Suddenly, I felt relief he pulled out but I had no idea what was about to happen would be worse. He practically dragged me to the bedroom. Once in there he threw me on the bed and put his hands around my throat and began to choke and fuck me at the same time. I could barely breathe in that moment and I felt like I was going to die.

Letting out a loud roar he slowly took his hands from around my throat, and eased off me.

Coughing and gasping for air, once I caught my breathe I screamed at him "What the fuck is wrong with you? Were you trying to kill me?"

This asshole looks at me with a dead pan face and says "no I was fucking you."

How would anyone react to what just happened? Basically this man just rapped me and almost chocked me to death. With nothing to say I jumped up and ran to the shower.

Standing in the hot water I start crying and scrub his

smell off of me. How could he treat and talk to me like this? I thought he loved me. I made a mistake by moving in with him. I'm out of here in the morning. I don't care where I go but I won't be staying here. Memories flood my mind from when I was younger around twelve. I was raped by my stepfather. He always had an excuse to have sex with me. He would say things like "Let me check to see if it's right down there." Then say "you better not tell anyone and I mean no one." He always waited for my mother to leave out the house for bingo to start messing with me. I hated it, and I hated that my mom left me in the house with him.

Although she didn't have a clue, I still blamed her a little. I tried to give out clues, but she never caught on. His words danced in my head "You better not tell anyone." Always making me think he's going to hurt me if I did.

Imagine being twelve and going through all of this and no one to turn to because you were afraid of what might happen. Imagine hating yourself because you were too weak to stop it, hating yourself for being afraid. Afraid of what people would think, afraid that my mother would blame me and say I asked for it.

I hated my stepfather, I wanted him to die so bad that it consumed me every thought.

Finally, I had to tell myself it wasn't my fault that he repeatedly raped me, I never wanted this. He was sick in the head and I had enough of feeling like I was nothing, so I went to my mom and told her about what was happening. It was so comforting when she sided with me and got rid of his ass. My fears were just that, fears. My mother blamed him and held no ill feeling towards me for his actions.

I never understood how people could say they love you, but have no problem treating you like nothing.

Finished with my shower and tears, I dried up and step out the bathroom, Startled because this mother fucker was standing right outside the door as soon as I opened it.

I looked at him with such distain and pushed passed him "Move". Finding an outfit he started talking "I'm sorry baby. I'm just having a bad day. I could lose everything. I'm stressed out. Please forgive me I took my anger out on you and that was wrong."

"I understand but Leon you were wrong for this. I never thought that you would act this way. I think I should move out." "Move out? I said I'm sorry and it won't happen again. I love you baby please forgive me." "I love you too." Taking me by my hands, he kisses me on my lips and I let him.

What the hell is wrong with me? Looking at him in the eyes I said "I accept your apology but please don't ever do that again." "I won't". Really wanting to believe him I decide to make dinner.

The whole time he kept apologizing and kissing me. I couldn't help but love his stupid ass and together we sat to enjoy dinner.

Chapter Ten

The verbal and physical abuse continues

His promise to never do it again didn't even last two months. He started right back up again and it only got worse. I was trying to leave he pulled me back in the door and broke my index finger.

It's astonishing how a man can hit you and call you out your name but yet act so innocent and be so apologetic. I'm so sick of this shit.

Hell my friend Tammy tried to come over to see me. This man has the nerve to tell me no company today like I'm a child. Like really, I haven't had company in a minute. The worst part is I sent her away so I wouldn't get in trouble.

It's not my fault that he lost all his licenses. I've been doing my best to help. My store isn't making the money like it used to and every penny is going on the bills since he ran out of money. It's not like he's out there trying to find a job either. Every other day he needs money for something. My funds are almost cleaned out as well.

"Aja" Oh God here he comes again "Aja.". "Yes Leon!" "Where's the fucking pants that I had lying on the chair in the bedroom". Nervous about what is going to happen I say "Babe, I put it in the wash." "Did I fucking ask you to wash them?" "No but"... "But nothing my ass, don't touch anything unless you ask me first." I should have just agreed and walked away but no me being me I just had to keep talking. "Leon, come on now you're taking this a bit too far don't you think." "Really, Aja too far, I will take it how far as I want and if you don't shut your mouth you'll see how far I'll take it. Get your ass up and go and make me something to eat."

Walking away my mouth continues even after hit threat. "Why you got to be so mean to me? I'm doing everything I can to help the both of us out. It's like my best isn't good enough for you." "Don't question me, just get your ass in the kitchen and start putting some food in them pots. I better smell something soon."

This time I just zipped my lips. I didn't want to hear him talk anymore. Sometimes I just want to hit him up side his head with a frying pan and knock his ass the fuck out.

I'm not stupid or blind I know Leon has become physically and emotionally abusive since we moved in together but I love him. I know I've got to get away from this man, but I think "Maybe if I just do as he says, we wouldn't have these problems." I know I'm defending his actions by taking the blame but that's what happens when you repeat a pattern.

Deflated and stressed I yell for him "Babe your food is ready." He storms into the kitchen and plops down on the chair "It's about dam time. You had me waiting long enough." Just as he put his fork into his food he looked at me and asked "what the fuck is this?" "Chicken and dumplings I thought I'd Make something different for you." "Did I ask for you to try something different? You know what the fuck I like and it isn't any fucking chicken and dumplings." "But babe", as soon as I said babe, he got up and threw his food on the floor and told me to eat it.

Not saying a word I grabbed the kitchen rag so I could clean up the mess but before I could start he said "Since you want to cook me dog food now you get on your knees and eat like a dog"

My eyes quickly filled with tears "What?" I asked with glossy eyes. "Don't what me. Just do what the fuck I tell you." My mind was all over the place, the tears began falling from my eyes and soft whimpers exited my mouth.

"Did I shudder?" He moved behind me and pulled me by my hair and threw me on the floor. He forcefully pushed my face in the food like a dog smelling his own shit. "Now eat it with no hands!!" Crying uncontrollably now, I grabbed some food. Just as I was about to put some in my mouth he punched me in the back of my head and told me to "never make this shit again."

I couldn't believe this man was making me eat off the floor like it was ok. When he finally walked out the kitchen the flood gates opened. I sit there crying like I lost my dearest friend. While I sat there and tried to compose myself I heard the car drive off.

In all my years I don't believe I ever moved that fast.

Running to the room, I quickly began packing my stuff so I can get the fuck away from here. On my way down the stairs I grabbed my purse and keys and out the door I went. Before I had my keys in the ignition this nigga pulled back in the driveway and blocked me in. There's only one way in and out of here and now I'm trapped by a 2000lb vehicle and an abusive bastard.

Quickly I locked my doors and rolled up my window. Jumping out of his car I could hear my name as he got closer "Aja, Aja" Shaking in my seat he looked at me through the window. "Where do you think you're going?"

Feeling a little safer behind my locked car door I said "I'm getting the fuck away from you all you've been doing is abusing me." "Look I'm sorry, I know I lose my mind sometimes." "No you're not! If you were sorry you wouldn't hit me and now you're going to lose your girl."

I could see the rage building in him as he grabbed in the door handle and tried to get in. "Leon, just move your truck so I can leave." "I'm not moving shit." "If you don't move I'm going to call the cops on you." "Call the cops you won't live to tell about it." "What?" That's when he pulled his gun out. "Now open the fucking door before I put one in your head."

As soon as I unlocked the door he pulled it open and put the gun to my head and said "if you ever try this shit again, the next time anyone sees you will be at your funeral." Snatching me out of the car he slapped me in my face hard. So hard it felt like he punched me instead. What dark eyes he told me to get my ass in the house and get myself together.

Entering the house I headed straight to the bathroom.

My sobbing wouldn't stop. Tears and snot just kept flowing like a broken faucet. I used so much tissue that my nose was red and raw. For the first time today I looked at the women looking back at me in the mirror and I couldn't believe what I was seeing.

Looking at my face it was unrecognizable. I was no longer the beautiful, well put together lady I remembered. My face was bloody and swollen and the headache that was starting to set in caused me to cry again.

Running the sink water I grabbed a wash cloth to clean my face. The moment the cloth and water touched my face the pain was excruciating. What little strength I had left gave way and I Dropped to my knees. Crying in pain I asked God "Why? Why me God? What did I do to deserve this kind of abuse?"

I knew I should have stuck to my guns and never fooled around with anyone from the club. I just knew it. I'm so stupid and why the heck did I listen to my friend.

This isn't Love at all. He can't possibly love me and treat me like I'm some slave or an animal. I got to come up with some type of plan to get out of this. Meanwhile I have to stay chill.

Just as I regained my bearings and stood up there was a knock at the door. "Are you done in there yet?" I'll be out soon, I'm about to get in the shower." "Good girl, that's right wash that pussy so I can get some."

This nigga has lost his fucking mind. He really thinks that after slapping me and putting a gun to my head that I'm going to have sex with him. "Hell no, Not tonight my head hurts."

He busted in the bathroom door and grabbed me by

my throat. "I told you about telling me no. If you don't give me some I'm going to take it and after I take it, I'm going to whoop your ass. So what's it going to be?"

Crying "ok, ok, I'll be in the room once I get done." "No bitch you're done now. He pulled me all the way to the room and told me to lie down and he jumped on top of me and started fucking the shit out me.

At that moment I wanted to die. I didn't want to live anymore. I wished at that moment that he would have shot me and ended this torture. Never in a million years did I think I'd end up with someone who treated me like this. This had to be a nightmare, and I was waiting for someone to wake me up. This isn't my life, this can't be my life.

I'm supposed to be happy like I was before. Now this man is beating on me, rapping me, verbally and emotionally abusing me. I'm twelve all over again. Hating myself and blaming myself for this.

Over and over I repeated to myself "Please hurry up and get the fuck off me." I could feel and smell his hot funky breath on my face and the pain I was experiencing was so intense that I wanted to vomit.

In all my years I would never put disgusted and overjoyed together when it came to sex, fucking, rape or love making but when Leon whispered I'm Cumming, it was like music to my ears.

I didn't want him on me or inside of me. As soon as he rolled off me I got up and walked towards the door. Breathing heavy with a sound of satisfaction he said "don't try no funny shit. I'll get you."

Ignoring him and his threat I walked in the bathroom, locked the door behind me and jumped in the shower.

As I scrubbed and scrubbed between my legs to get his scent of me I tried to think of ways to get away from him. I have to ask for help somehow, before it's too late.

Once I walked in the room this nigga hurried up and get off the phone. So I asked him "Who was that?" and as expected he said "None of your business. So you better not touch my phone or else I'm going to kick your ass." And with that statement he walks out of the room.

Hmmmm another women I thought to myself. Well, He won't have to worry about killing me because I'm going to kill him if it is.

Exhausted and hurt I say nothing more. Right now I can't even think straight my head still hurts from that hit. I'll deal with this shit later after I sleep this headache away.

Chapter Eleven

The heat is on

As the dim light from outside my window cascades shadows on the ceiling I lay here in my bed. My thoughts are consumed with the drama from yesterday. The shock and fear that I felt threaten to take over and almost bring me to tears. Flashes of my life flicker before my eyes. The question dances in my head like a bad rock and roll song, who makes someone eat off the floor and puts a gun to their head? "Leon does" the small timid voice in my head says.

Now this whole dam phone situation is another matter. I know dam well if it was a family member or one of his boys he would have stayed on the phone talking shit, but to rush off the way he did, yea ok that was another female.

This Negro has me twisted. Yeah I admit he's abusing me and spending all my money but I'm about to get detective on his ass, especially since he won't let me go. Yea mother fucker shits about to hit the fan.

Taking a deep breath to relax my nerves, I get up and

ready for work. Making my way down stairs I can smell bacon in the air and noise coming from the kitchen. I walk down the short hall and enter the kitchen to find Leon making breakfast.

He raises his face to look at me and smiles "Good morning" he said as he came over and kissed me on my cheeks. Overwhelmed with disgust every fiber of my being wanted to scream in his face "what's so good about it?" but I didn't, I just said "good morning."

As he turned to walk away he said "I'm making my favorite lady in the world, the love of my life some breakfast."

If there was such a thing as Super powers I would have picked lasers in my eyes because if looks could kill, he would have been dead right then and there.

Standing there just starting at him with pure hatred coursing through my body he said "Have a seat babe, I made you some bacon, eggs, grits with cheese in it, and some homemade biscuits." Just as he turned to me I gave off a look like I was happy, but inside I felt pure unadulterated rage setting in. With a big smile I said "thank you babe, I appreciate this." Although I was pissed off I was also hungry and I couldn't wait to dig in. It felt like a Double edge sword at this moment, anger or hunger. I love me some good breakfast so my stomach won. Lol!

Gathering up my first bite I looked across the table at his stupid ass and I couldn't understand why he was so happy all of a sudden. Before I could eat a second bite he began to talk "You know babe I just want to apologize to you about yesterday. The thought of losing you forever just took my mind over. I don't want to lose you. I love you so much. I just couldn't see you without me in your life."

Slowly losing my appetite I hear each and every bull shit word that he is saying 'Hear' is the operative word because I'm sure as hell not listening. My thoughts are talking over his and saying "Negro please shut the fuck up. I'm so tired of these apologies, and then you turn right back around and do the same shit over again. That's all I ever hear nowadays, I'm sorry, I'm so sorry. Yea you're sorry alright, Sorry looking." What the hell I wish he just get the fuck out of my face already.

Wanting him to shut and allowing my curiosity get the best of me; I cut him off "Babe you seem to be in a good mood this morning is there something going on?" "No babe!! I'm just happy that God gave me another day to get it right." Every muscle in my stomach tensed and I had to hold back the vomit that threatened to expel from my mouth. Did this abuser just say "God" Like he even knows the work of God. This character is a joker!! Trying not to lose my shit and scream "Did God tell you to hit me and treat me like this? HELL no he didn't." I looked down at my plate and took a long deep breath. Quicker then I should have I started shoving food in my mouth to block those words from escaping, until his cell started ringing.

Unable to control my curiosity my eyes quickly went to his screen but before I could focus on the name he snatched it off the table and walked into the next room.

Pissed at his reaction I quietly slid my chair away from the table and began to stand. Once I heard him say hello, I quickly tip toed over to the door so is be able to hear what he was saying, and how he was saying it.

Trying to keep my composure as I ease drop on his conversation I heard him say "She's about to leave for work in a half. Lunch! Ok I can meet you there at noon. Don't worry it's on me. Ok babes see you soon."

Outraged and furious I rushed back to my chair and pretended I was eating. I couldn't believe what I just heard. This Fucking asshole has his nerve, Not only has he been abusing me, but now's he's fucking cheating and spending my money on another bitch.

My heart was racing; I felt my mind swimming in a fog so thick that I felt like throwing up. I could not believe this shit. After I've been busting my ass trying to make ends meet. Hell no! I'm not here to support him and his side hoes.

Right then is when my crazy broke free; I was plotting to murder his ass. Crazy thoughts began swimming in my head, like feeding his ass rat poison, maybe tying his ass to the bed while he slept and waking him up with a pair scissors open around his dick ready to clip it off and shove it down his fucking throat.

I quickly snapped out of my crazy when he sat next to me talking. Again trying to compose my inner rage I asked "who was that babe?" Holy shit why did he just say "my homeboy Troy" I almost lost my shit, this man knows he can lie. Before I spoke I forcefully swallowed back the viscous words screaming to escape and said "Oh ok so what are you guys doing today?" "Well he has to work, but we're planning on a trip for next month." "Oh ok!" I said as I stood up from my chair and began to walk over to the sink. I turned to look at him and he seemed pleased with his attempt of deception.

So instead of playing along with his bull shit lie any longer, I asked as calmly as possible "So are you cheating on me with your boy." The color of his eyes looked black as coal in that moment. It's like I had awoken the devil and he was ready to attack.

He jumped off his chair like a predictor about to attack its prey, "Hell no! Why would you ask some stupid shit like that? I'm not into guys have you lost your mind."

Even though it was my intentions too piss him off I was nerves. Calmly, tempting my luck to see if he'll lie again I said "Well you just said you were speaking to Troy, right?" moving closer to me he said "Yea dumb ass that's what I said. Now why would you ask some ignorant shit like that?"

With an internal smile of victory I said "Maybe your conversation. Ok babe, she leaves in a half, lunch at noon, it's on me. Now if that was Troy like you said I think you need to re-evaluate your life choices, unless of course you were lying and it was a female on the other line."

Lord knows I wish there was a hidden camera at that very moment. His face was like a cartoon of different emotions. Shock, anger, confusion, disbelief and I'd be dammed even glee. Like this mother fucker was happy about being caught in a lie.

Extremely concerned with his final expression I gradually began to move out of his space. The tone of his voice made every hair on my body rise like when a cat hackles. "Aja are you ease dropping on my conversations now? You don't have trust in me?"

Walking and talking at the same time I continued with "Leon, how can I believe you when you're always hitting me, calling me names, you treat me like a door mate, like I'm nothing just something to walk over and clean off the bottom of your shoes. You say you love me but your actions tell me something else. So yes I am asking you, are you cheating on me? because I know dam well that wasn't Troy. So please don't try and play with my intelligence."

The look on his face answered my question before he even spoke. Yes he's cheating and yes he was about to lie again. "Aja, why would I do that? I'm not trying to lose you. That was my cousin. I told her I'd take her out to eat. She's been going through something's." "Ok" I said, "I got to get to work. I'll see you later. Have a good day babe." The look of nervousness was all over his face. Not to mention, the sweat on his forehead was like he was working out in 95 degree weather.

Once outside, the wind blew across my face as if it knew I needed to calm down. I was so mad and upset, that I hadn't realized I was all sweaty.

The cool breeze caused goose pimples up my arms and neck.

Something was wrong I could feel it in my gut. It pulled at my insides. Screaming and fighting for me to listen. My momma always said, to go with your gut feeling because it was usually right.

My fingers quickly began to dial my friend Tammy before I jumped in my truck.

"Ring, Ring, and Ring" The ringing was deathly loud in my ears, smothering the sound of my rapid beating heart. My emotions we're on overload Anxiety, frustration, anger, betrayal, hurt and most of all disdain. At this very moment I loathe Leon with every fiber of my being.

"DAM IT PICK UP" just as I was about to hang up I heard "Hey girl! What you up to?"

It's nice having friends your man isn't too familiar with, my girl Tammy just got a new Lexus, so he won't know what her ride looks like. After giving her a quick rundown of the bull shit I ask her if I can borrow her car around 11 this morning for about an hour so I can find out what the hell is going on.

My girl never lets me down without further question she said "Ok, I'll meet you at your store at 10:30a." "Ok cool! See you then and we can talk some more later.

Pulling into my store parking lot, I see Sarah standing there attached to her phone waiting to get in. She finally raises her head long enough to notice me walking up. "Good morning, Miss Aja!" "Good Morning Sarah".

Walking into the store, I turn to Sarah and tell her "I need to make a run around 11 this morning, but if anyone calls me, tell them I'm busy with inventory, and I'll call them back. I don't care who it is. I'm busy!!" With a look of concern she stopped to look at me "Ok Miss Aja, Is everything ok?" "Yes! I just need to take care of something, nothing to be concerned about". As I make my way to my office I turn back in the direction I left Sarah. "One more thing Sarah, my friend Tammy will be here around 10:30 just send her to my office". "Ok Miss Aja" "Thank you!"

Entering my office I feel my nerves begin to tie in a knot. You know the feeling bubble guts. What if I get there and find out that it is another woman. What will I do or say? Dam it I hate feeling this way.

Trying not to hyperventilate I take a few deep breaths and exhale slowly. I can't worry about this right now. It's time to get my detective on.

Just as I finish throwing on my jeans, sneakers and hat on my girlfriend Tammy walks in the door. "Aja, what are you about to do and why are you dressed like that?" "Like I said earlier I need to take care of some business". "I know you need to find out some shit but" her face contorted when she looked me in the face "What's wrong with your face, Aja? Is that Negro putting his hands on you? What are you planning"?

Trying to cover my face with my hair and hold back tears, Tammy walks over hugs me, and begins crying. Hugging her back I hold strong like a statue and assure her that I'm fine, but I need to leave out right now.

Without hesitation she says "Do you need me to come with you?" Man she really is my ride or die chic. I love that she's willing to be by my side knowing that I'm about you act a fool. "No Tammy I just need you to stay here. But if you need to leave here's my truck keys. I'll call you soon". Quickly I hug her and rush out door.

CHAPTER TWELVE

The Heat continues

Rushing out the door I hop into Tammy's Lexus and floor the gas pedal and had do for the highway. Speeding down the passing lane hitting a speed of 85 miles per hour, I pray I make it home in time so I can follow Leon.

My increased anxiety is threatening to get the best of me, my nerves are shaken and my heart is pounding like it wants to break free from my chest, but I can't let that stop me now.

Needing to find out the truth I inhale deeply and exhale slowly to calm myself. Mildly relaxed I realize I'm a couple minutes from our house. A block away I become more aware of the passing cars. I take quick glances when they pass, I don't want to miss this a-hole.

Finally, I make a right down our street and decide it's best for me to park a few doors down just so he doesn't spot me.

I'm relieved to spot his car still in the drive way and by

the looks of it I made it just in time, Leon started to back out the drive way.

Dam it he's heading in my direction so I ease down in the seat so he doesn't spot me as he passes.

Looking in my rear view mirror to spot his car I quickly make a U-turn making sure that I don't get to close, I stay three cars back.

Driving and talking to myself until my phone rings. It was Tammy, so I answer.

Before I good say hello i hear her yell on the line "Girl you ok?" "Tammy look I'm good. I'll call you back as soon as I can." Quickly I hung the phone up.

Still a few cars behind Leon I have an idea where he's going and sure enough I was right. I spotted an unfamiliar restaurant just a couple blocks ahead.

Leon turns into the restaurant parking lot and you know I sure followed. I wonder what the hell they sell here with a name called, 'We Cook Great Food'. Sounds like a lie to me especially if it needs to broadcasted in the title.

Parking at least 10 cars down the row, I watch him go in. I gave it about 10 minutes before I went in. Let's just say that was no small feat for me. I was ready to go in once the door closed behind him. My nerves were all over the place and at this point truth be told I just didn't care. Once in the restaurant I noticed he's already been seated with his "Cousin". Wink, Wink cousin my ass.

They sat in the far corner, his back was to me so instead of losing my shit right then I decided to have a seat and order a coffee. I'm going to do some surveillance and see how this plays out.

The restaurant smells of southern cooking. The smell

of colic greens and fried chicken dance in the air. Hell if I wasn't on a mission I'd definitely order a meal. The restaurant is almost full with couples enjoying their meals and you can hear children laughing in one of the booths. You can tell this place has been around a while nothing appears too updated. It has a feeling of home and togetherness, It actually quite relaxing.

An older lady named Sue brings my coffee and I thank her. She looks like life has handed her the shaft but she still lives and loves with 100%.

Focused and determined now I return my eyes to the corner. I see them talking and I can almost distinguish her laugh from the others. My blood is at a low boil but I'm chilling. I'm not sure how much longer I sat there and just watched them talk and laugh but once I saw them hug and kiss let's just say the Cuckoo Bird flew out the Cuckoo's nest.

My ass flew up out my seat so dam fast that I'm sure I seen the lady in the booth startle and jump. My cuckoo went hell-a crazy. I made it over to his table in record time and slapped the shit out of her, and punch him in his mother fucking face.

All reasoning was gone; I had no filter and began to scream at the top of my lungs. I'm sure every person in that placed stopped to watch.

"HOW COULD YOU?? You sit here and beat on me, take my money and you have the fucking nerve to cheat on me, you fucking low class of a man."

Through the ringing in my ears I hear this chick screaming "bitch you hit me?" Turning my face to hers I yell "Yesssss bitch and I will do it again if you don't sit your clown ass down, looking like he picked you up from the side of the road."

At this point my adrenaline level was so high I could feel myself shaking. Not because I was scared but because I was truly hoping this bitch would try me. I'm a grown ass women and I haven't wanted to kick someone's ass as bad as I did at that very moment.

It wasn't even a few seconds later when I felt Leon's hand on my shoulder as he turned me around and jump in my face, yelling at me, then he hit me. Shocked and stunned I blinked a few times. My first thought was "Why can't believe this mother fucker just did that."

I don't know where my man balls grew from, but I slapped his ass right across his face and before he could react people came running over to calm me down. Which in turn pissed me off more? What was wrong with these people his ass was the one cheating.

These mother fuckers had the nerve to throw me out of the restaurant like I care, hell I'm sure I cook great food too way better than them.

Once outside the cool breeze his me and my nerves started to settle. Jumping in the car I head back to my store. I'm sure my blood pressure is through the roof and I can feel a headache coming.

I barley put the car in park when Tammy ass runs out the door. She must been sitting at the window like a stalker waiting for me to pull up. "Girl what happen? Are you ok? Why your hair a mess? Girl what did you do?" The look I gave her said if you don't let me get inside this store I may loss my shit. She was about to keep asking questions so I just walked passed her into the store.

It took me a few minutes to compose myself and just as I was about to talk, I heard my store door slam and Leon yelling. "Aja, Aja, where are you?" Tammy's face paled when I looked at her.

I walked out around the corner and that's when I seen him walking towards me. Still feeling pumped I said "I'm here, what the fuck you want?" His eyes were black as coil when I looked in them "What the fuck I want" he said. This is when I spotted him pull his fist back to punch me, I moved to the side and started running until I fell on the floor. Of course this was the end of the fight he sat on top of me and began to hit me then choke me, I tried fighting him back but it became hard to breath and things started to turn dark. The last thing I remember was hearing Tammy and Sarah screaming.

I'm not sure how much time passed but when I woke up I was in the hospital. I could hear Tammy and my mom praying over me. The lights were so bright I had to squint. "Mom" I said. "What's going on?" I could feel my mother's warm hand grab mine "Oh baby you've been unconscious for two days." My head still felt a little foggy "What are you talking about?"

Even though I couldn't open my eyes fully I knew she began to cry. "Baby he beat, he beat you so, so bad." Tammy chimed in at this point "Aja, he choked you till you were almost dead." mom spoke a little stronger this time. "Baby, Tammy called the cops just in time. If she didn't, you wouldn't be here right now, both of them hugged me.

I knew I shouldn't ask but I did all the same "Where is he now?" Silence swallowed the room. It felt like forever before they answered. Then with a strained voiced my mother finally spoke "Baby, we don't know, once he heard the cop cars he ran. Right now just focus on getting better." I'm not sure what my facial expression was because let's be honest I couldn't feel it. I'm sure I did something because I heard Tammy snicker.

"Does one of you have a mirror?" In unison they both said "NO" liars I'm sure they just don't want me to see my face. "I need help to the bathroom. Can one of you help me? Tammy helps walk me to the bathroom." I definitely was aware enough to know; I was way too weak and doped up to make it on my own.

My legs felt like hundred pound boulders as I made my way to the bathroom. I'm pretty sure I just dragged my feet across the cold floor.

Looking in the mirror I couldn't even recognize myself. Tears fell from my eyes like rain falls from the heavens. Shaking my head in disbelief I cried out "God, Why?"

Ladies, This man beat me so bad that my face is swollen, I have two black eyes, both my lips are busted open and even though you may not see it he has taken a piece of who I am and destroyed it.

Chapter Thirteen

The rage

Rage and revenge consume me. My thoughts revolve around all the crazy things I want to do, and what I'm going to do to him. Visions of Leon beating me, belittling me, cheating on me and dam near killing me invade my sleep and most of the hours I'm awake.

I've been out of the hospital for about three days now and still haven't been to the store. It's been closed for about two weeks. Hell, I still need more time to get better and heal my face completely.

Dazed and in deep thought the phone ringing brings me back from the revenge zone, but when I look down at my phone, and it's this ass hole calling and texting me, flames burn inside me like a ravaging forest fire.

Is he FUCKING serious right now? Reading his text messages I'm outraged at how ballsy he is. This Negro must have fell and hit his head. He really has some nerve. Talking about "I'm sorry can we please talk". I'm not paying his ass any attention and as of right now I'm not answering his calls.

Feeling frustrated and tired I decide to get some rest. The medication they put me on makes me feel woozy and like shit. In fact as of today I'm not taking them anymore. Finally, resting my eyes I think to myself I'll have to talk to him soon. I need to get my stuff out of his house. Not just yet though, I need to rest.

Waking around 7pm I can see my phone notification light blinking like a disco ball. This man has called me 10 times and texted me about 20 times. I know he just won't stop. So emotionally defeated I decided to pick up the phone and call him back.

It wasn't even a full ring before he picked it up. "Aja, baby I'm so sorry. Please forgive me baby, come back home." Taken back by his urgency and pleading of words, I just breathe. "Aja, are still there?" "Leon, I'm not coming back to you. I just need to get my belongings from your house." "You mean our house", he says. "No, it's your house and this here is way too much. I just need my stuff". Still pleading Leon ask again "Please, Can you come over so we can talk face to face. I promise I will keep my hands to myself." "Leon, you've told me that time and time again and I just don't believe you anymore". "Please, Aja baby one more chance".

I do need to get my things I said to myself, so I agreed to stop by. However I did call Tammy to let her know my plans. She didn't want me to go, but I had too. Of course I didn't tell my mom because I'm a hundred percent she'll start tripping.

Grabbing a knife and my pepper spray before I leave,

I tuck them safely in my purse; you know just in case this fucker decides to show his ass again. Hey you never know.

After what felt like a life time I reached Leon's house, and as I pull up I spot him standing there with a bouquet of roses. Shaking my head I think "Please!! He could have saved that money. Hell he is going to need it.

My body tenses as I watch him walk up to my car and reach to open the door for me. Gently he took me by the hand and helped me out my truck.

All my senses were on high alert. What is this guy p too and why the hell is acting so gentle and loving. With his sweetest voice and most seductive smile he placed the flowers in my hand and said "these are for you". Every hair on my body stood straight. I had no words so I just looked at them.

As we walked up to the house, the silence was eerie like a horror movie. You know what I mean. The scene is set, menacing music plays in the back ground and you know you should run but you have to know what happens next and there's always that one stupid brood that runs to the danger. Yeah right now my life feels like that movie and I'm yelling at the screen "run Bitch, don't do it, just run".

Once at the door I took a deep breath and swallowed hard. Leon opened the door and it was like being in the past. Not one shred of electricity being used. The whole house was lite by candle light, rose petals covered the floor as far as I could see.

It's amazing the lengths a man will go to when he's done wrong to a good women. This gesture would have been romantic under different circumstances. Shit, I would have jumped his bones right then and there, but life isn't a romantic love story.

Heartbroken, I looked at him and said, "This is nice but I'm just here to talk and get my belonging that's it".

Without saying a word he took me by my hand and sat me by the fireplace and grabbed a bottle of wine. Frustrated and angry with his sudden nicety's I asked "Leon what is all of this about?"

Just then Leon turns to Hand me a full glass of wine and I refuse by saying "I can't drink I'm on medication, Thanks to you!" Setting down the drinks he drops to his knees and folds my hands in his. "I'm sorry baby!! Please forgive me. I'm begging for our forgiveness. I'm so sorry"

My heart wants to believe him, wants to forgive him, wants to love him, but my brain Is screaming "HELL NO". Remember what he did to you, how he treated you, and most importantly how he dam near killed you.

With a heavy heart and as much strength as I could muster in that moment I said, "Leon you hurt me too many times and you always say you're sorry but always do it again. I've done everything in my power for you and you've treated me like garbage more times then I care to remember. You beat me down and broke my will then still had the audacity to turn around and cheat. Answer me this Leon, how long have you been cheating on me?"

I honestly didn't expect him to answer but when he did, the bullshit that came out made me want to punch him in his mouth. This ass hole had the balls to say "I just started; I didn't feel like a man anymore, you were doing everything, so I needed a woman to need me, because it felt like you didn't."

Are you FUCKING kidding me right now? This is the most ridiculous shit I've ever heard. Is this man seriously trying to make this shit my fault? What a poor ass excuse of a man.

Without losing my shit I said "You know what, I need to get going, and I'm going to grab some of my things and head out." Before I could stand he said "Wait, I'm not finish talking to you, I still have something to say."

Still on his one knee, he reached into his pocket and pulled out a box "Aja, Will you marry me?"

Disgust and disbelief wrap around me like a cloud of smoke. How in the fuck did this Negro get money for this ring when he has been claiming for months that he's broke? I've been paying for all these fucking bills, holding his ass down, and he has enough money to buy a ring. I almost lost my store while I was the only one holding us down. I can't believe this low life mother fucker. Not once did he offer to help me when I was down. I told him time and time again that my business was in trouble but he acted like he didn't hear a word I said. Now all of a sudden, he has money for a ring!

The ring in his hand was beautiful It had to cost anywhere between 3 to 5 thousand dollars.

My blood began to boil and I could feel the pressure in my head begin to build. I could feel myself about to lose my temper. Opening my eyes I looked at him and calmly replied with "We're not ready for this." His eyes looked crazy, not black and empty but off somehow. This is when I felt him squeeze my fingers just enough for me to notice and he said "Come on, Aja! We can work through this."

Feeling nervous and unsure of how to answer, my jaw

tensed and through tightened teeth I said again "Leon, we're not ready for this." I could feel my hands begin to sweat as my temperature began to rise, feel my chest begin to tighten as my nerves began to quiver and bile rise in the back of my throat as I realized coming here was a horrible mistake.

I was given every indication of what was about to go down. It was just a matter of time but my unconditional love, devotion and fear for him has brought me back.

Chapter Fourteen

The Rage Continues

As I sit here and stare at this man, I can't believe he's still fucking begging me to marry him. I can hear my heart beat pounding in my ears. I'm sure my blood pressure is off the charts right now.

My heart and mind are at odds, but my rage has taken control. The only thing I want to do to him right now is to beat the shit out of him just like he did me. I'm going to get his ass the question is how am I going to do that? Think fast and smart Aja, I say to myself. I got it!!

I was so deep in my mind I forgot Leon was still begging for my hand in marriage, scheming my revenge I smiled at him as sweet as possible and said "yes, I will marry you".

The weight of the ring on my finger was overwhelming. I felt like being shackled to a ten ton anchor. Just the mere feel of it threatened to stop my breath as my chest tightened.

This moment would be the most important act of my

life; I had to keep my emotions in check. Pretending to be happy I told him "I forgive him".

What happened next made me vomit in my mouth a little. He started to put his disgusting lips on my neck, and mouth. Thank God for simple favors, it was my neck first or I would have vomited right in his fucking mouth.

The way he's touching and feeling me, I already know he's going to want some pussy. So I decided to help him want this pussy, because this will be the last time he'd want anyone's pussy again.

I can feel his dick getting hard as hell as he presses it up against my ass. So to move this along, I begin grinding forcefully on his dick because I know that's how he likes it. Just as expected I hear him let out a low moan.

With a victory grin I took his hand and lead the way to the bedroom. Piece by piece I began to remove his cloths while rubbing my hand on his dick. I pushed him down on the bed while I climbed on top of him. Kissing and grinding on him until I put his dick inside my pussy. Fucking the shit out of him till he tried to get on top. Once he said baby let me fuck you from behind, with a small grin on my face I quickly replied by saying, baby tonight is all about you besides Baby, I want to try some new things with you tonight, since we're engaged to be marry. His sudden excitement was palpable.

"Oh yeah, what's that?" Leon asked. "I want to get real freaky baby. I want to tie you up and suck you, and fuck you, till you can't take it no more". "Why you want to tie me up?" Sensing his hesitation I turned up the charm. "Because baby then you can't stop me from fucking you the way I want to. After that you can do the same to me, deal??"

Son of a Bitch my plan is working I seen it in his eyes as soon as I said deal. "Sounds like a plan baby, but when it's my turn, I'm going to have your ass screaming." With a half-smile and a victory tone blasting in my brain, I thought to myself, you won't be getting that chance you fucking ass hole.

"I'll be right back baby, don't move." I slowly got up from the bed and headed downstairs to the basement. While getting the rope to tie him up to the bed, I noticed a baseball bat and decided it may come in handy. Of course the bat did not make its way to the bedroom but I did set it behind the couch so that he wouldn't notice it.

Back in the bedroom he was still lying there with his dick hard just waiting. Man I hate this mother fucker right now, but I gotta do what I gotta do.

Slowly and seductively I started to kiss him. Taking one hand after the other I tied each of them up to the bed rail. I continued kissing him all the way down to his feet. I tied them both one by one to the bed as well.

"Dam Aja it's kind of tight". "Awww baby you'll be alright. Just sit back and enjoy the ride". I climbed back on top of him placing his dick back inside of me, Keeping his mind free, and his body craving for more. I made sure to take my time fucking him. As soon as he told me that he was about to cum. I quickly jumped off of him.

With want and longing he said "Baby what you doing? I was about to cum, stop playing and get back on this dick and ride me". With satisfaction I got close to him and whispered in his ear "Who's playing baby?" A little more aggressive with his tone now "Aja would you stop, you got me horny as hell". "Oh do I?" I replied in my nice sexy voice," Hell yeah babe."

Sauntering over to the wall to turn on the big light I said to Leon "I want you to see all of me baby". His clueless ass was all excited. I could hear this fool talking about "what you doing babe?" "I'm going to the bathroom, I'll be right back".

As quickly as possible I ran into the other room where my clothes were at and put on my sweat clothes, socks and sneakers. I ran down to the living room to get the baseball bat and Grabbed my pepper spray before walking back into the bedroom.

The look on Leon's face when I entered the room was so satisfying, I could have probably left then and been happy but I didn't. "What the Fuck are you doing?" Walking close to the bed swing the bat around I said, "Leon what the fuck do you think I'm doing?" I could hear the uncertainty and mild fear in his voice. "Babe stop playing untie me"." No!! Your sorry ass is going to lay right there".

Pacing back and forth at the end of the bed he began screaming for me to untie him, all I can do was laugh my ass off. I'm sure by this time I had a crazy look going on.

Standing next to him now, I looked at him and said "Who's the bitch now? Scream as loud as you can, no one is coming. Look at my fucking face you miserable bastard. Do you see what the fuck you did? You took my money, you beat me up, made me eat off the floor like I was a dog, you put me in the hospital, not to mention, you cheated on me. Don't you know that karma is a bitch?"

"Aja I'm sorry, I'm so sorry forgive me please". "Forgive you" I looked him in his eyes with a straight face and said "this is a day you will never forget". I took the bat and hit the lamp and broke it. Screaming out loud in a rage of anger, "everything that I paid for, you will no longer have. I'm breaking your shit up, as well you mother fucker."

Yelling and crying like a baby he begged for me to stop. I could hear his pleads but my brain was set to revenge and destruction. I continued to break everything that was glass and anything breakable. Frustrated with his endless howling I turned around and began to yell at him.

"Man up you bitch ass. Only bitches hit on women. Tonight I'm going to make you my bitch. Now shut the fuck up before I hit you over the head with this bat". This is the moment I noticed his face was wet "Aww are you really crying tears? Did you fucking care about my pain, the hurt that you put me through?" "Yes!!" he said. Laughing I leaned in close "No you fucking didn't. Shut the fuck up and stop all that crying you bitch ass nigga."

Determined to continue with my destruction I left the bedroom and went through the rest of the house where I broke everything that I could. I pulled pictures off the wall, Jumped on them, and screamed "I hate you, I hate you".

With nothing left to break I went back into the bedroom and headed straight for his prized possessions. Yes ladies his gear. I sauntered right into his walk in closet and pulled all his clothes and shoes out and placed them in one big pile in the middle of the floor. The look in his eyes was of pure terror. He knew what was about to happen but was helpless as a child to stop it.

I could hear this fool screaming, begging for forgiveness as I walked down to the laundry room. I grabbed both bottles of bleach and strolled right back in the room, paused but for a second just to smile at him and poured them all over his clothes and shoes.

This feeling of control was just as good as an orgasm. Hell in some ways it was better. His crying now turned to a gasping whimper. You would have thought he lost his best friend by the way he was caring on.

Starring at him I thought "Man the way he's acting is really starting to piss me off more than I expected. I have no more patience for his cry baby ass". It's time.

Walking over to him with the pepper spray in my hand I looked at him and said, "There's nothing like a women scorned", and sprayed him right in his eyes.

Screaming, yelling, crying and begging for me to stop. I took the bat and hit him across his chest. Then I hit him in both of his knees real hard so that he wouldn't be able to walk again. As he cried out In pain, bleeding out his mouth and still begging me to stop I asked him, "how does it feels to beg a person to stop mistreating you, and they still keep doing it? Doesn't feel so good does it?"

"No, no I'm sorry, I'm sorry". "You are sorry, A sorry excuse a man. This is your lesson to learn how to treat a woman, especially a good one who helped you and did the best she could to keep not only herself, but also your ass a float when shit got rough. You have to learn you can't go around using, abusing and mistreating people who you claim to love and who have your back. I'm leaving now you fucking jackass. Have a great fucking night".

As I walked out the door, I felt just a little bad for him.

Ha, who was I kidding no I really didn't but I was feeling mildly guilty. If I let him lay there he might die. If I call for help, I'm going to jail. Hmmm which one is better? Jail or let him die. Fuck that shit. Let his ass die.

Well Needless to say, I'm in jail serving time. They gave me 5 years for attempted man slaughter. The neighbor heard him screaming for help. It's funny how the victim who fights back gets time, while the abuser gets away with it.

As for Leon, yeah I broke his knee caps. I heard he's trying to walk again. They said I broke a couple of his ribs when I hit him in his chest, Big deal, I should have wacked him a few more times. Hopefully he won't mistreat another women again in his life.

There are two lessons to be learned from this story: One There's nothing like a woman scorned and Two Karma will come back and get you.

So be careful how you treat people. What's that saying, treat people, how you want to be treated.

The End

Love

Love is beautiful,
Love is kind,
Love is loving without conditions, even in our hardest times.
Love is laughter, and sometimes tears,
Love is about balance and giving up some of your time.

Love is not running away in our struggles
But knowing how to handle one another
Pulling close, instead of away.
Not ashamed to say you're afraid.

Love is deep,
Love is free,
Love is you and me.

Dawna Durham

Crisis Services

24-Hour Crisis Hotline
716-834-3131

24-Hour Addiction Open Access Hotline
716-831-7007

24-Hour Chautauqua County Hotline
1-800-724-0461

24-Hour Erie County Domestic Violence Hotline
716-862-HELP (4357)

24-Hour Kid's Helpline
716-834-1144

24-Hour NYS Domestic & Sexual Violence Hotline
1-800-942-6906

www.crisisservices.org

About the Author

Dawna Durham mother of four lives in Buffalo, NY, but was born in Poughkeepsie, NY. She has written several plays such as, Love Hurts, Forgive me Beloved, The Nursing Home, and Love at last. In which she received a Proclamation from the Mayor in Niagara Falls, NY in 2011 for her play, Love Hurts, which is about Domestic violence.

Dawna herself had experienced domestic violence at a young age. Not only that, she lost a close friend to it as well. Dawna is one of the most humble, smart, talented women that I ever met. Her drive, and passion for helping others is a gift in itself.

Printed in the United States
By Bookmasters